E NERGY," SAYS FRANK EINSTEIN, KID GENIUS AND INVENTOR. "Power that can be converted into motion, light, heat—energy in all its different forms! That's what this is all about, Watson."

"MMMmphh mmm rrrmmm mmm," answers Watson.

Frank nods. "Oh yes. Of course—also forces. The way energy is applied. The way energy works in the world. Absolutely right, Watson."

Watson wiggles. "Rrrrarr rrrr ruuhhhh ruhhhh!"

Frank Einstein scratches his head with an oversized metal finger. "Oh yeah! This is the perfect chance to test my **HYPOTHESIS** . . . and the ultimate challenge for my Electro-Finger invention."

Watson, lashed to the front of a rubber raft drifting ever faster toward a roaring sound at the base of the dam in the river, would like to say, "Einstein, this is it! I'm done! You're crazy. This is *not* the perfect chance to test *anything*! And: HELLLLLLLP!"

But Watson can't say any of that.

Because Watson is not only taped to the raft.

His mouth is also duct-taped completely shut.

So all he can do is wiggle, bug his eyes out, and make noises.

"**We are presently moving quickly toward a column of water being sucked under the dam,**" says Klink.

"**Uh-oh,**" says Klank.

# FRANKEINSTEIN

## and the Electro-Finger

# JON SCIESZKA
### ILLUSTRATED BY BRIAN BIGGS

**AMULET BOOKS**
**LONDON**

**S**hurt . . . very much."

"It's the 'very much' that worries me," answers Watson, trying not to flinch.

Frank shuffles his feet on the wool rug. He raises his index finger until it's level with Watson's nose.

Klink, plugged into an outlet in a corner of Frank's laboratory, looks up and says, without any excitement, "Oh, how exciting. I cannot guess what is going to happen."

**"Me either! Me either! Me either!"** beeps Klank.

Klink turns his single camera eye to Klank. "I know exactly what is going to happen."

**"What?"** beeps Klank.

"What?" says Watson.

Frank moves his finger closer to Watson's face.

A tiny bolt of electricity jumps from Frank's finger to Watson's nose.

*Bzzzzzzt!*

"Yow!" yells Watson.

"Success!" cheers Frank.

**"Ha-ha-ha,"** beeps Klank.

`"And people call you a genius?"` says Klink.

Watson rubs his nose and sits back down at Frank's lab table. "What did you do that for?"

Frank adds a drawing and a quick note to his lab notebook. "Energy. Static electricity. The same thing as lightning, just on a smaller scale."

"So you lightning-bolted my nose?"

"Yes."

"Why?"

"Why do we do anything, Watson?" Frank pins a photo of a lightning strike up on the Wall of Science under *energy*. "To find out how things work. To make our next

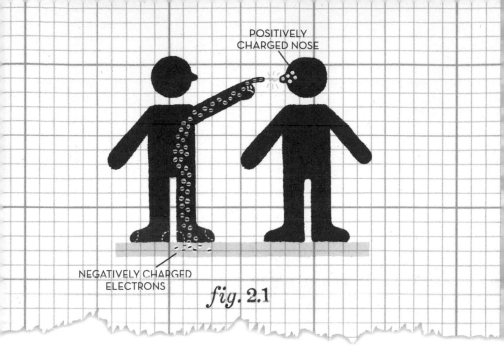

POSITIVELY CHARGED NOSE

NEGATIVELY CHARGED ELECTRONS

*fig.* **2.1**

invention. To get started on figuring out energy. But mostly to make you jump."

Klink unplugs his recharged self and autowinds his cord.

"Static electricity," Klink explains. "Free electrons gathered from rubbing the wool rug are negatively charged. They jumped to Watson's positively charged nose because the opposite charges attract."

"Which is exactly like lightning," explains Frank. "Storm clouds become negatively charged on the bottom. The lightning is the electricity discharging to the positive ground. Opposite charges attracting."

"So . . . great," says Watson. "You can make an invention to shock everyone's nose?"

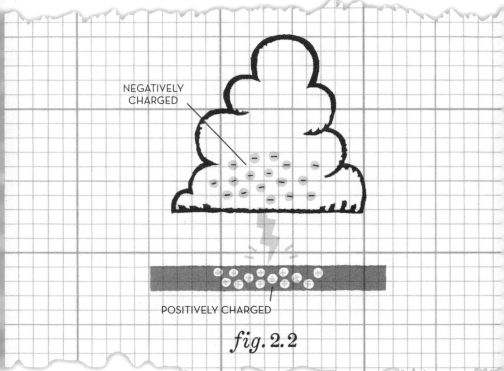

NEGATIVELY CHARGED

POSITIVELY CHARGED

*fig.* 2.2

"Oh, no," says Frank. "This is about *all* energy! And energy for all. Energy is what makes everything in the world go. Without energy, nothing would happen."

"This is true," says Klink. "Energy comes in many

different forms. You may be interested to see that I have improved myself with all-new energy attachments." Klink shows off his newest additions.

"Mechanical. Electrical. Magnetic. Chemical. Light. Heat. Nuclear. I did not add sound energy."

**"Yeah, yeah, yeah,"** says Klank. **"Because I have the sound energy. I am making a new Robot Boogie. Listen!**

**"Badang badang badang . . ."**

"Perfect!" says Frank. "All forms of energy. But the most completely amazing fact about energy is that it cannot be created or destroyed. It can only change from one form to another."

"Hmmm," says Watson, clearly not that amazed. "And how does any of this help me with *my* new invention?" Watson fiddles with a pile of tiny paper balls, dried peas, and BBs, searching for ones that fit nicely inside his big plastic straw.

Watson fits a pea into the opening. He blows a quick puff of air and shoots the pea at an empty soda can that he has set up as a target. The pea curves wildly and *pings!* off Klank's metal-canister body.

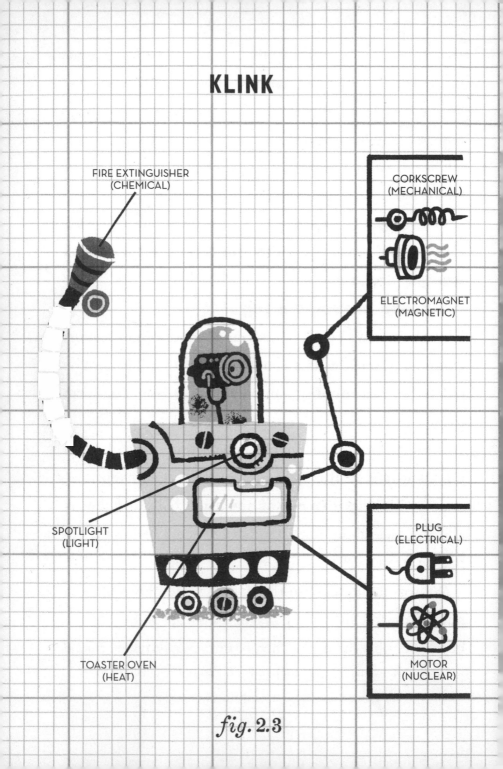

KLINK

FIRE EXTINGUISHER
(CHEMICAL)

CORKSCREW
(MECHANICAL)

ELECTROMAGNET
(MAGNETIC)

SPOTLIGHT
(LIGHT)

PLUG
(ELECTRICAL)

TOASTER OVEN
(HEAT)

MOTOR
(NUCLEAR)

*fig. 2.3*

"This is exactly what we're working on!" says Frank. "Forces. Forces are how energy is applied in the world. Forces are how motion happens. And a lot of that was figured out by this guy." Frank points to his Wall of Science. "Maybe the most famous scientist ever—

Sir Isaac Newton. He figured out the

Three Laws of Motion."

"Nice hair," says Watson.

"And we can use these laws about forces . . ."

While Frank is talking, Watson loads a small plastic BB into his shooter. He aims at a metal pipe on the ceiling.

". . . to direct the energy that—"

The BB misses the pipe and hits an aluminum duct—*tink!*

And suddenly a loud *CREAK THUMP BOOM* fills the laboratory. The walls shake. A whole section of the ceiling collapses and crashes to the concrete floor in a huge tangle of splintered wood and metal pipes.

"I didn't do it!" yells Watson. He looks at his peashooter. "*Did* I do it?"

But before anyone can say anything else, a hulking figure with massive arms and a sinister, hooded head rises out of the mess, croaking, moaning . . .

"It's going to attack!" yells Watson. "Everyone duck!"

Everyone ducks.

2

"A RRRGGGHHH," GROANS THE DARK SHAPE IN THE LABORATORY- dust cloud.

**"What is that?"** says Klank. **"I am afraid."**

"You cannot be afraid," says Klink. "You are a machine."

The menacing shape aims what looks like a bazooka on its shoulder.

**"OK,"** says Klank, dimly lit by his head antenna bulb. **"Maybe I am just very nervous."**

Frank grabs a steel pipe. He hands Watson a baseball bat. "We outnumber whoever or *whatever* it is. Charge on three. One . . ."

"What?" whispers Watson. "Maybe I should use my peashooter again instead."

"Two . . ."

The dark figure shakes itself, moans again, and points its bazooka cannon right at Klank.

**"Do not shoot!"** beeps Klank. **"I am a friendly machine."**

"Wha—? Huh?" says the dark shape in the dust. "Oh, sorry, fellas. I didn't mean to interrupt your chin-wagging confab."

"Grampa Al!" says Frank, dropping his steel pipe.

And it *is* Grampa Al. Because who else would ever say "chin-wagging confab"?

Grampa Al shrugs the ripped piece of canvas off his head. He pushes the busted pipe off his shoulder and kicks his way through the rubble of the collapsed roof.

"Doodlebugs! I forgot all about that patched piece of roof. Fell through and pulled my whole windmill construction right down with me."

Frank helps Grampa Al dust himself off. "Windmill? What are you doing with a windmill?"

Grampa Al sits down at the lab table. "Making my own

energy. Getting off the grid. Midville Power and Light is under new management. And they're sending electricity prices sky-high."

"We were just talking about energy," says Frank.

"And forces," adds Watson.

"Let me show you what I got. Maybe you guys can help." Grampa Al shuffles back to the pile of roof and windmill pieces. He pulls out a rolled-up piece of paper and lays out a blueprint of his building.

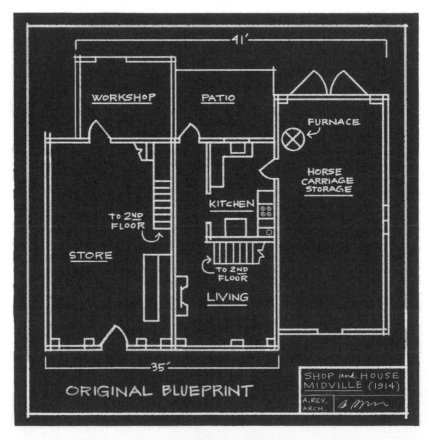

ORIGINAL BLUEPRINT

Grampa Al traces a path through the blueprint. "This is where the electric runs. This place is a hundred years old. It was built when there was plenty of coal, and oil was cheap. All its electricity came from burning those fossil fuels."

"Nonrenewable energy sources," says Klink, projecting a diagram onto one of Frank's laboratory walls.

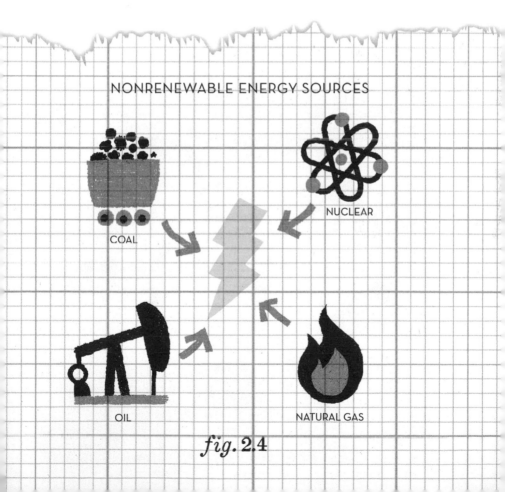

NONRENEWABLE ENERGY SOURCES

COAL

NUCLEAR

OIL

NATURAL GAS

*fig.* 2.4

"Plant and animal forms squashed and decaying over millions of years," says Klink. "Turned into coal and oil and gas."

"Exactly," says Grampa Al. "So I'm thinking we switch over to renewable energy."

Frank nods. "Stuff that doesn't take millions of years to replace."

Klink projects another diagram onto the wall.

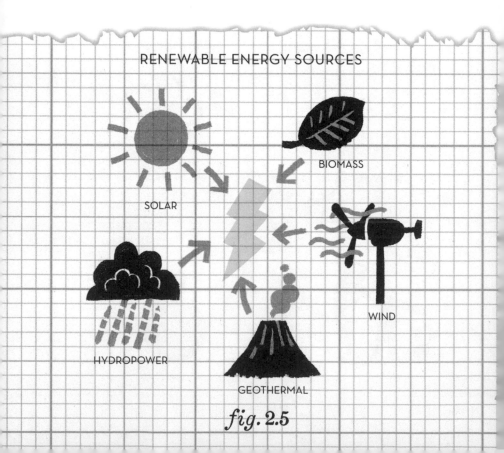

RENEWABLE ENERGY SOURCES

SOLAR

BIOMASS

WIND

HYDROPOWER

GEOTHERMAL

*fig. 2.5*

"Nice," says Frank. "Like geothermal energy—using the Earth's temperature to cool water in the summer, and heat water in the winter."

"And electricity generated from the windmill I was putting up top," says Grampa Al.

"And who knows what else? Maybe a solar-powered phone? A hydro-turbine-powered television set?" adds Frank.

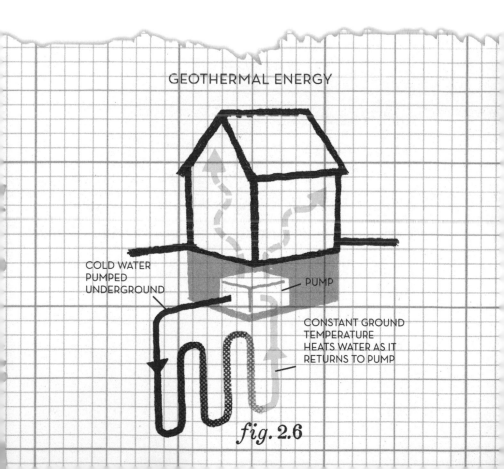

GEOTHERMAL ENERGY

COLD WATER PUMPED UNDERGROUND

PUMP

CONSTANT GROUND TEMPERATURE HEATS WATER AS IT RETURNS TO PUMP

*fig.* 2.6

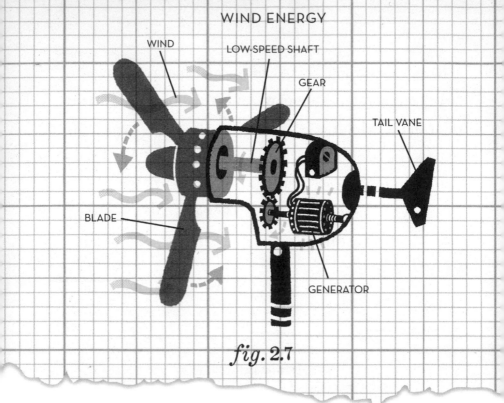

## WIND ENERGY

WIND

LOW-SPEED SHAFT

GEAR

TAIL VANE

BLADE

GENERATOR

*fig.* 2.7

"Cool," says Watson.

Frank studies the plans. Scratches his head. And nods. "Very cool. But you know what would be even cooler?"

**"A polar bear in a snowstorm?"** asks Klank.

"Even better than getting *off* the grid? Doing *without* a grid." Frank thinks out loud. "Totally wireless power. Available everywhere. No generators. No wires. Just tapping into the electrical power that is in the entire universe."

Frank points to another picture on the Wall of Science.

"There was a scientist named Nikola Tesla who lived around 1900 and did some amazing experiments with wireless energy. He thought it could be done."

"But that's impossible," says Watson.

Frank shuffles across his rug, lifts one finger, and—*bzzzzzzt*—zaps Watson's nose.

"Not really . . ." says Frank.

3

tip shoes, a floppy bow tie, and a bad haircut stands on top of the dam at the western end of Lake Midville.

The way he is waving his arms up and down, it's hard to tell if he is happy or angry or both.

But he is definitely talking to the chimpanzee standing next to him. The chimpanzee wearing pin-striped pants, a white shirt, a dark tie, and no shoes.

"I'm still mad at you for running off and letting Frank Einstein and his idiot robots wreck my Antimatter Motor," says the kid with the bad haircut, T. Edison. "But I have to say—your idea to buy the Midville Power and Light Company is pretty smart. For a monkey."

Mr. Chimp checks his phone, then puts it back in his pocket.

He gives Edison a sidelong glance and signs:

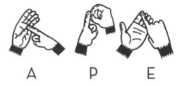

A      P      E

"Watch this," says Edison. He flips open the cover to the dam's control panel. He punches the green button under the label OPEN SLUICE GATE.

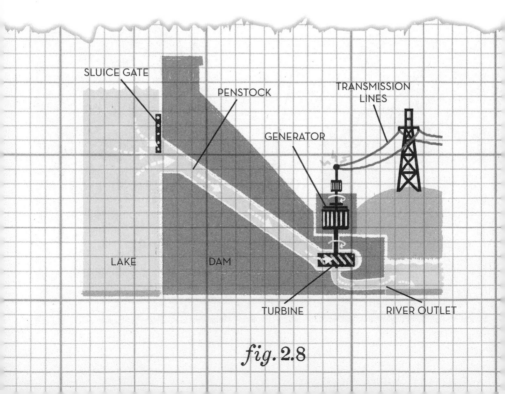

*fig.*2.8

Underwater, on the lake side of the concrete dam below their feet, an iron gate slides up with a low rumble and lets a rush of water thunder into the penstock tube.

Edison and Mr. Chimp watch the water in front of the dam swirl and form a gigantic whirlpool that disappears down under them.

"Pretty amazing, huh?" says Edison. "Nothing but moving water. Water that spins the turbine. Water that turns the electrical generator shaft. Water that sends electricity to the transformer. Water that delivers my electricity to my suckers ... oh, I mean customers. Customers who have to pay whatever I tell them to pay."

Mr. Chimp motions with two hands, as if throttling himself.

"Well, of course," says Edison. "Once we buy and close all the other electricity-producing companies, we will have the customers in a choke hold."

Edison and Mr. Chimp watch the dark whirlpool, feel the rumbling hum spin of the heavy metal turbine blades and shaft, imagine the electricity speeding through the wires.

Mr. Chimp draws his index finger slowly across his throat.

Edison leans back in surprise. "And then we kill everyone?!"

Mr. Chimp rolls his eyes. He frowns and shakes his head, as if to say, *No, you idiot. I just meant close the sluice gate.*

Mr. Chimp punches the red CLOSE SLUICE GATE button.

"Let's close the sluice gate," says Edison.

He doesn't see Mr. Chimp roll his eyes again.

Edison and Mr. Chimp head back to shore. Edison turns to look at what is now *his* hydroelectric dam.

"My plan will make all of Midville depend on me for all their energy!"

Mr. Chimp signs:

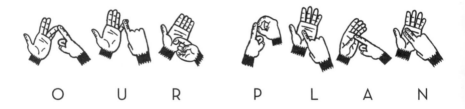

O   U   R   P   L   A   N

"Anyone who plugs in *anything* will have to pay me *everything*!"

Mr. Chimp cracks a nut, chews it, and signs:

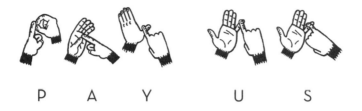

P    A    Y        U       S

"Yeah, yeah," says Edison.

The surface of Lake Midville is calm and quiet again.

Mr. Chimp chews his walnut thoughtfully, then nods.

## 4

FRANK CONTINUES, "AND SO TESLA FIGURED OUT THAT THERE might be a way to supply electricity, without wires, to anyone, anywhere in the world, much more cheaply than any power company could."

"Best thing since sliced bread," says Grampa Al. "You boys get crackin' on that wireless idea. I'm going to get my contraption spinning."

Grampa Al picks up his windmill pieces from the roof rubble and heads out the lab door.

Frank, Klink, and Klank clean up the rest of the mess.

"Watson," says Frank, "experiment time. Could you go into the kitchen and get one balloon, two packets of salt, three packets of pepper, and one plastic spoon?"

"That sounds about as scientific as . . . my peashooter," says Watson, heading for the kitchen as Frank and the robots finish cleaning up the lab.

Watson returns with the experiment supplies. "I can't wait to see what you make with this."

Frank rips open the salt and pepper packets and dumps everything into one pile on the table.

He blows up the balloon. "Rub this on your head, Watson."

Watson rubs the balloon on his head. "Oh, this is much more scientific."

"Just watch," says Frank. "Now put the balloon over the salt and pepper."

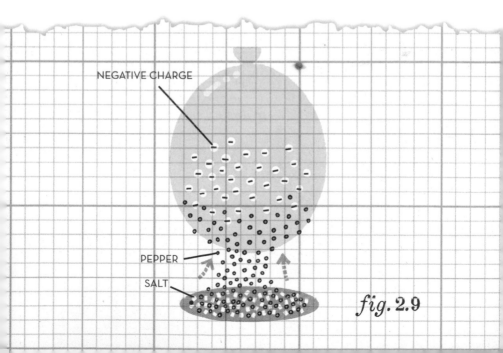

fig. 2.9

Watson moves the balloon. The positively charged, lighter pieces of pepper separate from the heavier pieces of salt and stick to the balloon.

"Wireless," says Frank. "And cheap. Now watch this." Frank rubs the plastic spoon on Watson's sweater.

He turns the water on in the lab sink so that a small, steady stream flows out.

"Observe."

Frank puts the spoon near the water column.

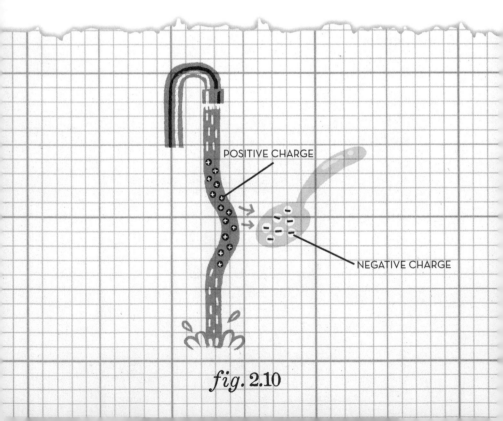

POSITIVE CHARGE

NEGATIVE CHARGE

*fig.* 2.10

"No way!" says Watson. "The water is bending toward the spoon!"

Klink beeps, "In both cases, extra negative charge caused by gathering electrons . . . attracts positively charged pepper pieces and water stream."

"How amazing would it be if energy were wireless? And free?" says Frank.

"My energy will be wireless electricity," says Klink.

**"My energy will be Robot Boogie sound,"** says Klank.

"My energy will be Watson's Perfect Peashooter," says Watson.

*Rrrraaarrrrrrrrrh!* roars the DimetrodonPhone in Grampa Al's kitchen. *Rrrraaarrrrrrrh!*

**5**

**F**RANK POKES THE DIMETRODON'S EYE TO ANSWER THE INCOMING call. A wavy video image of Bob and Mary Einstein, wearing matching red-plaid hunting caps, pops up on the Dimetrodon's dorsal-fin video screen.

"Hi, Mom. Hi, Dad."

"Check it out, son!" Bob waves his hand at the night sky behind him. It is lit with curtains of shimmering green and white light. "The northern lights!"

"Cool," says Frank. "Aurora borealis."

"A new friend of yours, sweetie?" asks Mary on the screen.

"No, Mom. 'Aurora borealis' is the scientific name for the northern lights."

Watson sits down at the kitchen table, fiddling with different projectiles for his peashooter. "Hi, Mr. and Mrs. Einstein. Where in the world are you guys now?"

Watson loads a spitball into his straw and shoots it at his target—an empty soda can—with a puff of air.

"Yellowknife!" says Bob. "Just four hundred kilometers from the Arctic Circle! Another great spot for us Travelalloverstheplace.com travelers."

Watson's spitball misses the soda can completely and splats against Klink's glass-dome head with a wet *plop*.

"Drat," says Watson.

"Yuck," says Klink.

**"Ha!"** says Klank.

"No—Canada!" Bob yells over a hiss of static.

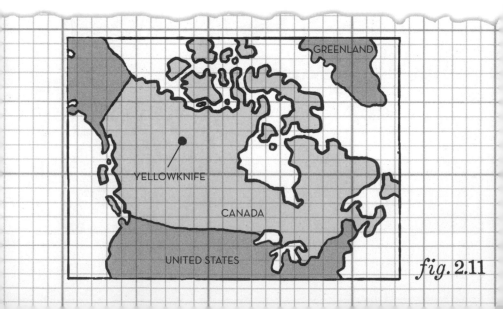

fig. 2.11

Mary Einstein waves. "Hello, Klink. Hello, Klank. I hope you're taking good care of my guys."

Klank waves back. **"Oh yes, we are. We must always protect our humans. And now we must learn everything about energy to be wireless."**

"Whaaaaat?" says Mary.

Klink wipes Watson's spitball off his dome with his squeegee attachment. "Even if those humans are—"

"You guys would love this!" yells Bob. "A fella up here was telling us the northern lights are all caused by solar wind, and how Earth is a magnet and—"

*Ssshhhhhhhhhhhhhhhhhh!*

A burst of static blots out both the sound and picture of Bob and Mary on the Dimetrodon screen.

Frank hangs up with another eye poke.

"More energy. It's everywhere," says Frank. "That static was probably caused by a solar flare's energy cutting off the phone transmission."

"Very likely," says Klink. "Because solar-flare energy is what causes the aurora borealis. Charged particles from the sun collide with gas atoms and

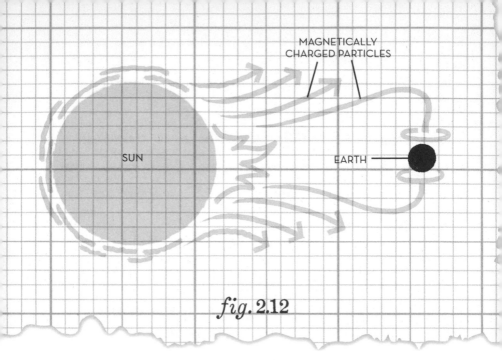

MAGNETICALLY CHARGED PARTICLES

SUN

EARTH

*fig.* 2.12

molecules in your planet's atmosphere, and emit different—colored light energy."

Watson loads a dried pea into his shooter. "But why do you have to go to the North Pole to see it?"

Watson blows another quick puff. This dried-pea bullet also misses its target and bounces off Klank with a metallic *ping!*

"The North and South Poles are the two places where the Earth's magnetic field is strongest," says Frank. "So that's where the solar wind/atmosphere collisions glow the most."

Watson twirls his peashooter. "The Earth is a magnet?"

"Exactly!" says Frank Einstein. "It has a magnetic north

NORTH
MAGNETIC POLE

SOUTH
MAGNETIC POLE

*fig.* 2.13

pole and south pole just like every magnet. It's what makes a compass work. The magnetic end of a compass needle points north."

Frank thinks:

*Magnetism comes from moving electrons.*

*Electrons that are moving in huge loops.*

*What are moving electrons called?*

*Electricity.*

*Invisible. Wireless. Electricity.*

Frank Einstein scratches his head, making his hair even messier than usual. "That gives me an idea. To the junkyard!"

6

chain swings away from the tall, striped, concrete smokestack next to the river.

Inside the crane, a long, hairy ape hand pushes the swing control lever left.

The thirty-meter boom of the crawler crane pivots left.

The wrecking ball stops at the top of its arc . . . then swings back, following the boom, and smashes into the last Midville Coal Plant smokestack with an earth-shaking *thump!*

The smokestack wobbles, tilts, and—*BOOM CRASH—* collapses in a heap of brick and concrete and old coal dust.

The entire Midville Coal Plant, which used to:

burn coal

    to

heat water into steam

    to

spin turbines

    to

run generators

    to

produce electricity

    to

send to transformers

    to

transmit electricity to half of the houses in Midville . . .

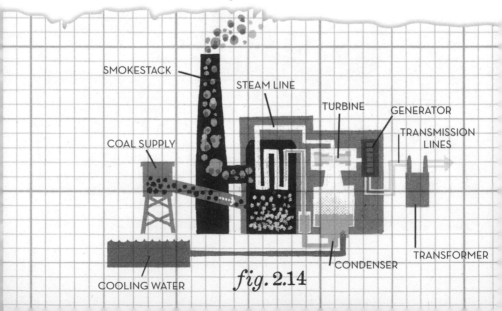

*fig.* 2.14

. . . is now a pile of rubble.

Mr. Chimp pushes his bright yellow hard hat back onto his head. He slaps the dashboard of the crane's control cab and hoots a pleased "Hoo-hoo-hoo."

T. Edison pulls a new notebook from the pocket of his orange safety vest and makes a very careful big black check mark.

"Midville Coal, done! Two more power plants left to smash. Then the only one working is my hydroelectric plant!"

Mr. Chimp backs up the crawler crane and puts it into PARK. He drops the two-ton wrecking ball to its cradle on the ground. He then shuts off the engine and signs:

O     U     R

Edison climbs down from the crane. "Our? What are you yapping about? Our *what*?"

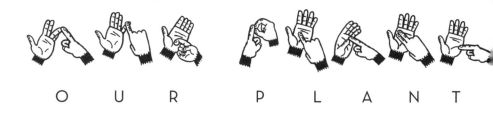

O     U     R          P     L     A     N     T

Edison waves his hand at Mr. Chimp.

Mr. Chimp does not like humans waving hands at him. He bark-screams a very loud *"Ooo-ooo-AAAAHHHH-AHHH!"* and slaps an open hand against his chest.

"Oh, fine. I know, I know. Half the power plant is yours."

Edison takes a rolled-up sign over to the fence surrounding the plant. "But this stroke of genius is all mine."

Edison unrolls the sign and ties it to the fence.

"We'll call it 'building,' but these idiots won't even understand that we are *destroying* everything except our power plant."

## 7

SITTING IN THE MIDDLE OF GRAMPA AL'S BACKYARD JUNK PILE, Frank Einstein consults his Energy notebook.

"Here are the basics we need to know," says Frank. He continues:

"Energy is all around us.

"Energy is what makes everything happen.

"Energy is a property of matter.

"Energy comes in many forms . . . like light, heat, sound, electrical, chemical, mechanical, and nuclear.

"Energy cannot be created or destroyed. But it can be transferred from one object to another. And it can be converted into different forms.

"And forces!" Frank adds. "Forces are the ways that

energy is applied. The pushes and the pulls that get things moving."

**"I have added jets to my legs to get things moving,"** says Klank. **"Watch!"**

Klank pushes a new green button on his side panel. Small rocket motors on the bottoms of his metal feet fire up with a low, roaring blowtorch sound.

Klank rises slowly up off the ground.

Watson checks the engines. "Saturn V F-1 booster rockets! Nice!"

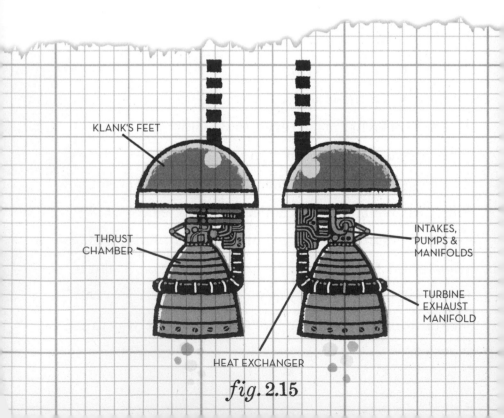

KLANK'S FEET

THRUST
CHAMBER

INTAKES,
PUMPS &
MANIFOLDS

TURBINE
EXHAUST
MANIFOLD

HEAT EXCHANGER

*fig.* 2.15

"Wow," says Frank.

Even Klink is impressed. "Very nice."

Klank rises higher. He turns his feet right and flies left. He turns his feet left and flies right.

"A perfect demonstration of all three of Newton's Laws of Motion!" says Frank.

"Huh?" says Klank.

Klank rises higher.

"One: An object at rest will stay at rest unless a force acts on it."

The tiny rockets roar a bit louder. Klank zigs and zags around the backyard a bit more wildly.

"Two: When a force acts on an object, that object will move, speed up, slow down, change direction. The greater the force, the greater the change of movement. What are you using to control the thrust?" asks Frank.

"What is that?" yells Klank.

"Thrust!" repeats Frank, now shouting above the building roar of the rockets. "The amount of energy the engines are pushing out!"

"OHHHhhhh," says Klank, bouncing off the brick wall

of the back of Grampa Al's Fix It! shop. **"I have not figured that ooooouuuuuutttt . . ."**

Klank's foot rockets erupt at full power.

Klank flies around the yard, bouncing off walls, fences, telephone poles, and wires. His legs flop. His legs twist. His legs wrap around each other. And he roars straight up into the sky.

"Three: For every action, there is an equal and opposite reaction," says Frank.

**"Heeeeeeelllllllp!"**

"Point your feet up!" yells Frank.

Klank points his feet up. He stops rising, turns in a big, jet-propelled curve, and rockets back down to earth, into Grampa Al's backyard, with a *SMASH BOOM BLAAAANG*, crushing three old metal file cabinets, a shopping cart, and a baby grand piano.

Klank's foot rockets sputter out and go quiet.

Klink rolls over to Klank and helps untwist his legs.

"Nice demonstration of Newton's Three Laws," says Watson.

*Phooomph!* goes one last blast of a rocket in Klank's left foot.

**"I am going back to a safer form of energy,"** says Klank. **"Badang badang. Badang a-lang a-ding dong. Boogie bing bong."**

"What?" says Watson.

**"Ding ding ding,"** plays Klank.

And Klank goes out.

8

and closes the big robot's foot-rocket panels. Klank helps, tightening his own bolts with his monkey-wrench hand.

Frank stands up and dusts off his lab coat. "OK, back to the Energy drawing board. Let's keep this simple."

"Yes," agrees Klink, showing off by blinking his new light-energy attachment. "As Sir Isaac Newton so simply put his Three Laws of Motion in his book *Philosophiæ Naturalis Principia Mathematica* . . ." Klink pauses and hums for a second. "Which I have just read. In the original Latin."

**"Ooh! Ooh!"** adds Klank. **"I am reading that, too."** He blinks his antenna bulb. **"And there is a piece of cheese on the basketball court, and if you touch it you get the Cheese Touch. It's like cooties."**

Klink whirs and searches his memory. "I do not see where Sir Isaac Newton wrote about the Cheese Touch . . . or the *Caseum Tago* . . ."

Watson laughs. "It's from the first *Diary of a Wimpy Kid*."

**"Yes!"** beeps Klank, waving his big duct-hose arms around. **"It is amazing! And Sir Isaac Newton is very good at drawing in that book, too."**

"No, no, no," protests Klink.

Watson nods. "Wait until you get to the end."

Klank stops moving. **"What? Does something bad happen? Something scary?"**

Klink hums and speed-reads from his library connection. "Rowley has to—"

"Don't tell him!" says Watson.

"Why not?" asks Klink.

"It's more fun to read it yourself."

"It is information. How can it be fun?"

"Because. It just is."

"Hmmmmmmmmm," fumes Klink.

Frank laughs. "I can't believe you guys are arguing about cheese. Klink, help us out with 'simple machines.'"

"Researching 'simple,'" says Klink. "Six simple machines: the simplest mechanisms that provide mechanical advantage . . . for you weak humans."

Watson eyes Klink. "That last bit doesn't sound like part of the definition."

Klink spins his webcam eye. "I added it because it is true. One: the inclined plane."

"Like a ramp," says Frank.

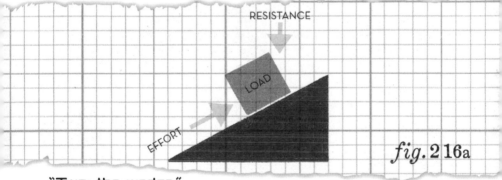

fig. 2.16a

"Two: the wedge."

"An ax," says Frank.

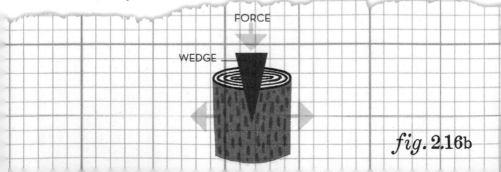

fig. 2.16b

"Three: the lever."

"Like a crowbar," says Watson.

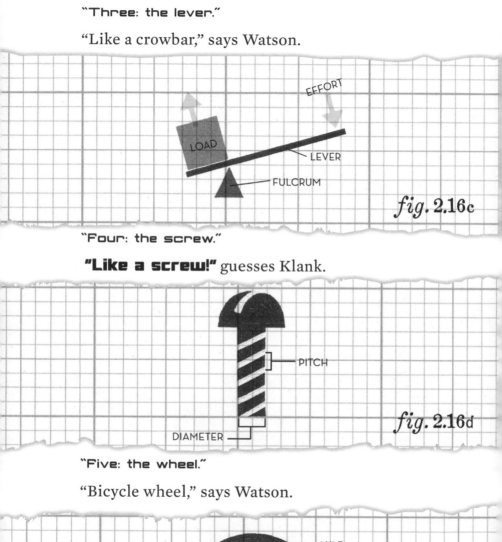

EFFORT

LOAD

LEVER

FULCRUM

*fig.* **2.16c**

"Four: the screw."

**"Like a screw!"** guesses Klank.

PITCH

DIAMETER

*fig.* **2.16d**

"Five: the wheel."

"Bicycle wheel," says Watson.

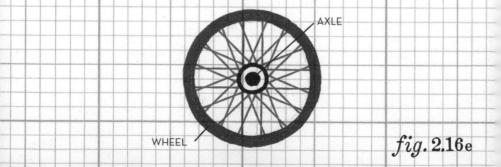

AXLE

WHEEL

*fig.* **2.16e**

"And six: the pulley."

"Like the pulleys in Grampa Al's dumbwaiter," says Frank.

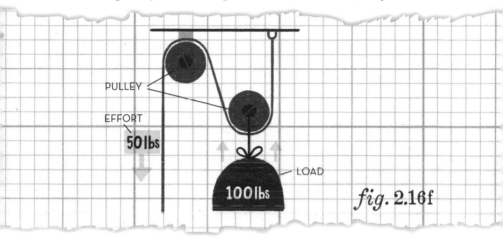

*fig.* 2.16f

"Those are all simple machines," says Frank. "And all great ways to increase mechanical power. But I was thinking—"

**"Hey!"** says Klank. **"Why did the simple machine throw the butter out the window?"**

"We do not have enough information to answer the question," says Klink, "but we may guess that the machine was built to throw butter."

Watson really wants to know. "Why *did* the simple machine throw the butter out the window?"

**"Because he wanted to see a butterfly!"**

"Whaaaaaa?" says Klink. "That cannot be true." Klink

shorts out and falls into his GPS glitch. *"Bzzzzzzzzt.*
*Recalculating route. Recalculating route."*

Watson and Klank laugh.

Frank shakes his head and tries not to laugh. But that is just not possible.

ment. "So here is the heart of the idea—electricity and magnetism are two different forms of the same thing."

"Electron energy," says Klink, holding up both his lightbulb and magnet attachments.

"Exactly," says Frank. "Electricity can make magnetism. And magnetism can make electricity."

"Like how chocolate milk is both chocolate and milk," adds Watson.

"No," says Frank Einstein. "Not at all like that. But interesting, Watson. Observe this experiment."

Frank picks up a big iron nail. He sticks it into a pile of paper clips, then pulls it out. "Just a plain old nail, right?"

"Right," says Watson.

Frank winds a copper wire around the nail.

"But if we wrap the iron nail in copper wire . . ."

Frank tapes one end of the wire to the top of a battery, the other end of the wire to the bottom.

". . . and run electrons from the battery through the wire . . ."

Frank sticks the nail into the pile of paper clips again.

". . . we make the nail into a magnet!"

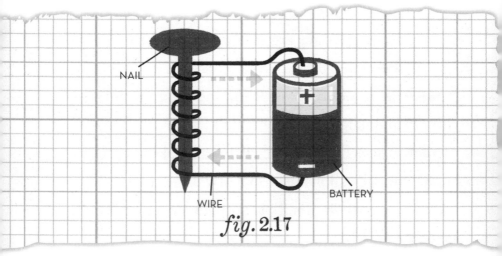

NAIL

WIRE

BATTERY

*fig.* 2.17

Frank lifts up the nail, this time dragging a bunch of paper clips with it.

"Magic!" says Watson.

"No—magnet," says Klink. "The electric current flowing through the wire produces a magnetic field around it. More wire makes a stronger field. So the electrified coiled wire makes a field just like a magnet."

Watson nods. "Magnetism from electricity."

"And now watch this!" says Frank.

Frank coils a longer copper wire in many big loops. He tapes one end of the wire to the side of the metal base of a small flashlight bulb. He tapes the other end of the wire to the tip of the bulb base.

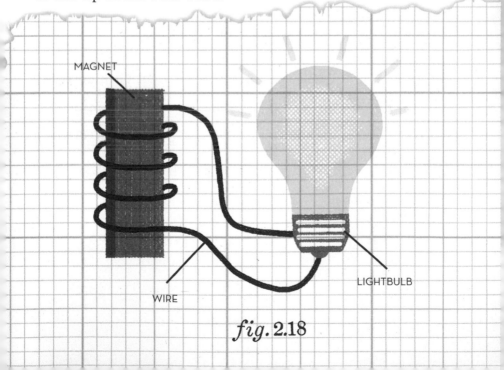

MAGNET

WIRE

LIGHTBULB

*fig.* 2.18

"This bulb needs electricity to light up," says Frank.

"Right," says Watson.

Frank picks up a bar magnet. "If you move a magnet in and out of the coils of the copper wire, it moves the electrons in the wire . . ."

Frank moves the magnet quickly in and out of the wire coils.

The bulb lights.

". . . and it makes electricity!"

"That is tooooo weird," marvels Watson. "Magnetism can make electricity. And electricity can make magnetism. But I guess that's right. 'Cause both are moving electrons around."

Frank jumps up from the lab bench. "And since Earth acts as a giant magnet, imagine how much electricity Earth could make. And imagine if we could tap into it anywhere. And shoot it out—*like a static-electricity finger!*"

10

**T**HE EVENING BREEZE BENDS THE TALL GRASS AT THE BASE OF the chain-link fence surrounding the Midville Wind Farm. The wind picks up, stirs leaves, bends branches, and pushes the giant fiberglass blades of a twenty-five-meter-tall white wind turbine into spinning motion.

The wind whips across the ridge above the Midville Woods and quickly sets the whole long line of windmill propellers spinning.

The spinning blades turn the shafts in the generators.

The turning shafts force electrons to move in an electric current.

Just inside the Midville Wind Farm fence, Mr. Chimp belts himself into the driver's seat of his latest machine. It's his own invention, the DemoMonster—with crushing jaws on a boom neck, and two extendable hammer arms.

Mr. Chimp signs to Edison:

B   U   C   K   L   E   U   P

"You are such an old lady, with your seat belts and safety helmets," says Edison. But he buckles his seat belt.

And it's a good thing he does. Because Mr. Chimp stomps on the gas, jams the crusher boom forward with a jolt, and crumples the first turbine shaft in its steel jaws with a shriek of ripping metal and crack of exploding concrete base.

Edison holds on to the sides of his seat, riding it like a bucking bronco.

"My goodness," says Edison.

Mr. Chimp's DemoMonster chomps and hammers and smashes and crashes one wind turbine after another.

Edison smiles more than he ever has.

"Oh my, oh my. Such destruction. No more electricity from this wind farm. Now that's what I call Building Our Future."

Mr. Chimp nods. Mr. Chimp hoots. Mr. Chimp sends another towering wind turbine crashing to earth.

**K**LANK BENDS THE LAST PIECE OF STEEL INTO PLACE.
Klink wraps wiring to match a Tesla diagram.

Frank locks the antenna into position.

Watson drills another soda can with his peashooter.

"Yes!" says Frank. He holds up his latest invention.
"The antenna will draw magnetic energy from the Earth
and pass it through the wire coils inside. Just like in our
experiment."

"Right," says Watson.

"Which will move the electrons in the wire coils to the
transformer."

"Check," says Watson.

"Which will shoot out of the fingertip transmitter. With no wires."

"Of course!" cheers Watson.

"Hold this lightbulb and stand over on the other side of the lab."

Watson picks up the oversized lightbulb and walks to the other side of the lab. "Why do you want me to—"

Frank aims the new invention at Watson.

"Hey, wait! No! Not me! This could be hazardous to my health! Make Klink hold it!"

Before Watson can move, Frank pulls the trigger. The lightbulb in Watson's hand flickers, hums, and then pops on in a bright white glow.

Watson stares at the bulb in his hand, which glows without being plugged into anything. "It . . . it works!"

"Of course it does," says Frank.

"Hypothesis tested and confirmed," adds Klink.

Klank shakes his big vegetable-strainer head. **"I did not think that was going to happen."**

Frank points the invention at an unplugged clock. The hands spin to life.

Frank electrifies a string of old Christmas-tree lights. They blink on and off.

Frank starts up a radio, a blender, a heater, and a fan. All wirelessly.

"Nice," says Watson. "What do you call it?"

Klink revs his vacuum motor. "It should obviously be

called the Wireless Electromagnetic-Transmission Device. Because that is precisely what it is."

**"Ooh, oooh,"** says Klank. **"You should call it . . . the Kooky Kootie Zapper!"**

"It's a real electro-finger," says Watson.

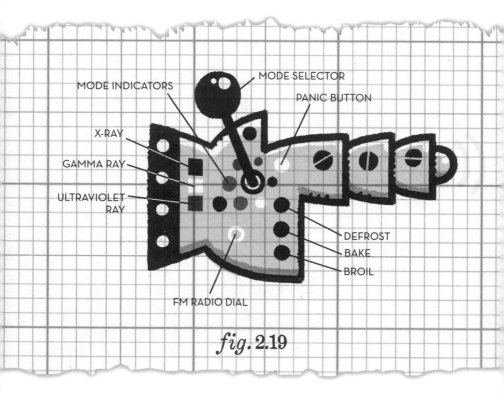

*fig.* **2.19**

Frank looks up. "Hey, that's a perfect name, Watson. Can we use it?"

Watson beams. He is thrilled to be part of Frank's invention. "Of course."

"Great," says Frank. "Now come on. Let's take this thing out and show Midville some wireless electricity."

Watson pauses. "Uh, Frank? Maybe we should think this thing through. Maybe make a plan so we don't get in trouble like we did last time. And the time before that. And the time before that."

Frank rummages behind his workbench. "Why do we need a plan? We are giving people free electricity."

"But what about . . . you know who?" Watson bends his head toward Klink and Klank.

Frank finds what he was looking for—an old purple-velvet-lined saxophone case. "Klink and Klank? Oh, absolutely. They have to help us, too."

"No, I mean—" Watson starts.

**"Hooray!"** booms Klank. He picks up Klink. He hugs Watson with one big metal arm. He squeezes Frank with another big metal arm. Klank spins everyone in circles, blasting his ROCK2 beat.

Klink beeps, "Blleeeeeeehhhhhhh!"

Frank and Watson spin around, yelling, "Ahhhhhhh-hhhhhhhhhhhhhhhh!"

Klank beats and spins and booms his crazy noises that sound like a washing machine screaming and a garbage disposal destroying a rocket engine.

Which is exactly why Frank and Watson's classmate and pal Janegoodall, on her way home from baseball practice, busts into the lab and starts smashing Klank all over his steel body, wiry legs, and metal-strainer head with perfect, sharp, fast strikes of her aluminum bat to save her friends.

three more fast strikes.

*WHAM! PING! DOINK!*

**"OOH! AHH! OWW!"**

"Janegoodall! Janegoodall!"

**"I am very delicate! Do not break my glass dome!"**

*BAM! BING! BOINK!*

**"OOO! OOO! OOO!"**

Klank drops Klink, Frank, and Watson in a heap. He hops around on one bent leg, covers his dented head with his twisted duct-hose arms, and dives under the workbench to save himself from the wild human smacking him with an aluminum bat.

Janegoodall cocks her bat for one more home-run swing.

"Wait!" yells Watson. "Don't hit him. That's Klank!"

"He's a robot," adds Frank. "Not a monster."

Janegoodall stops and looks over her shoulder.

Klink ducks behind Watson. "I am also not a monster. So you do not need to hit me, either."

Janegoodall lowers her bat, leans on it, and looks more closely at Klink and Klank. "Are you kidding me?"

Klink shakes and whirrs. "It is not possible for me to kid you."

Klank peeks out from under the workbench. **"I would hug you."**

"Well, I'll be . . ." says Janegoodall. "I was walking by, and it sounded like the world was ending in here. When I shoved in the side door, I thought you guys were getting mugged by that metal monster—I mean, Klank. So I thought I'd better take him down."

"Thanks for saving us," says Watson. "Even if we didn't need saving."

"Klank was just celebrating our newest invention," explains Frank.

Klank crawls out from under the workbench, nervously making sure the bench is between him and the new human.

Janegoodall nods. "Funny how celebrating and playing can look a lot like fighting. I've observed that in other species."

Watson notices that Klink and Klank are staying as far away from Janegoodall as possible. "These guys are amazing," he says. "Artificial intelligence, but they teach themselves. And they are constantly learning more and more."

"Really . . ." says Janegoodall.

"Most certainly," says Klink.

"Huh?" says Klank.

"Klink and Klank," says Frank Einstein, "meet our friend Janegoodall Jones. She is the best animal scientist and baseball player in all of Midville."

"You are Dr. Goodall? The famous chimpanzee scientist?"

Janegoodall laughs. "No. But my parents love her work. And they did name me after her. Nice to meet you."

Janegoodall reaches out and shakes Klink's vacuum-hose clamp-hand. Klank clomps over and gives her a hug.

"Sorry I smacked you around so much," says Janegoodall.

**"Oh, do not be sorry,"** says Klank. **"Nothing can hurt me."**

Klink looks at the dents all over Klank. "It did not help your looks."

Frank holds up the Electro-Finger. "We were just going to take the new invention out. Show the town of Midville that wireless power is possible with this."

Frank aims the Electro-Finger at the Christmas lights and flashes them on again.

Janegoodall takes the Electro-Finger from Frank and tries it out on the giant lightbulb. "Wow! Robots . . . wireless power . . . What next?" She removes her Midville Mud Hens baseball hat and shakes her hair out. "Frank Einstein, you are the craziest genius."

Frank smiles. He takes the Electro-Finger and packs it in the saxophone case. "We are going to show this to the world!"

"Uhhh, yes," says Watson. "But without freaking people out, or making them mad at us."

Janegoodall twists her hair, nodding and thinking. "Why don't you start at the band shell tonight? It's movie night. And everyone in Midville goes to movie night."

"That's perfect!" says Frank. "We can do a great demonstration by running the projector and the lights and everything electric . . . without wires. Who wouldn't like that?"

"I don't know," worries Watson. "I'm sure someone will hate us for something."

**"I do not want people to hate me,"** says Klank. **"I will hug them."**

"You cannot care," says Klink. "You are a robot. So please act like one."

Janegoodall yanks her Mud Hens cap back onto her head. "Haters are gonna hate. You can't live your life worried what people are going to think. Let's go crash movie night. They're showing one of those awful Tarzan movies. I'm adding it to my chimpanzee research project."

"Tarzan movie chimpanzee named Cheeta," says Klink, scanning online data. "Not one chimpanzee, but possibly as many as twelve different chimpanzees, and one boy human, over the course of filming, from the 1930s to the 1960s."

"One chimp or twelve," says Janegoodall, "that is just terrible that they had to perform in those movies. Chimps have families. They live almost as long as we do. They were prisoners."

Frank snaps the saxophone case shut. "OK, let's roll."

"Oh boy," sighs Watson.

"Beep-boop," says Klink.

**"Do-wacka-do,"** beats Klank.

Janegoodall shoulders her bat. "Light the way, Einstein. This is gonna be good."

# 13

. EDISON AND MR. CHIMP SIT QUIETLY ON A PICNIC BLANKET, perched on the ridge above the Midville Woods. A single cricket chirps in the fading light.

"Ahhhhh, Midville Wind Farm . . ."

T. Edison picks a daisy, sniffs it, then crushes it in one hand and throws it into the weeds above the line of shattered wind-turbine parts and broken blades.

". . . done!"

T. Edison pulls out his notebook and makes his second black check mark of the day. "Just the Midville Solar Array left."

T. Edison and Mr. Chimp look out over the motionless piles of Midville Wind Farm rubble.

The lone cricket rubs out one more weak chirp.

"Good work today, Mr. Chimp."

"*Oooh-ooh*," Mr. Chimp agrees.

"Let's celebrate."

T. Edison hands Mr. Chimp a brown paper bag with MR. CHIMP written on it. He opens the other bag, trying to hide the TOMMY written on the front.

"Mmm, let me see what we— Oh, yuck! Salami-and-banana sandwich? I hate salami and bananas!"

Mr. Chimp reaches into his bag and happily chomps his snack.

"What do you have?"

Mr. Chimp signs:

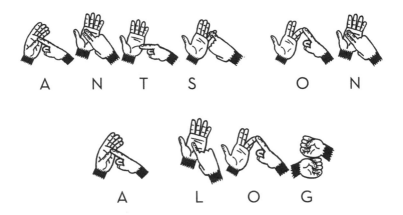

A  N  T  S    O  N

A    L    O    G

"Trade me," says T. Edison.

Mr. Chimp shakes his head no.

"You have to trade me. I'm your boss."

Mr. Chimp shakes his head again. He signs:

Y    O    U        W    O    N    '    T

L    I    K    E

"Don't tell me what I will like and won't like. I. Am. The. Boss. Trade me now!"

Mr. Chimp looks at T. Edison. Mr. Chimp likes bananas and he likes salami. Mr. Chimp shrugs and trades snack bags.

Edison grabs a stalk of peanut butter and raisin–filled celery and stuffs it into his mouth. "MMMrrrr rrrrummm ahhh," says T. Edison with his mouth full.

Mr. Chimp watches and waits.

T. Edison chews, stops, frowns, sticks his tongue out, and grabs something alive and wiggling in the half-chewed peanut butter and celery.

"BBBLLLAAAaaaaaaaaaaahhh!" screams T. Edison, jumping up and spitting everywhere.

"Bllaaaahh! Ptttwwaaaaa! Bluuuuhhh! *What* is *that?!*"

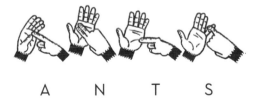

A    N    T    S

Mr. Chimp makes soft, short panting noises.

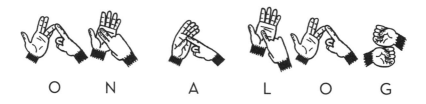

O N A L O G

"Ahhhhhhh! Yuck, yuck, yuck!" T. Edison stomps around the picnic blanket, still spitting. "OK, celebration over. Pack this stuff up, and let's get to movie night . . . for part two of our plan."

Mr. Chimp finishes his salami-and-banana sandwich in one giant chimpanzee bite. He wipes his lips with a paper napkin, folds it neatly, and tucks it into his pants pocket.

Mr. Chimp signs:

T A R Z A N ?

"It's always Tarzan."

And this makes Mr. Chimp both happy and sad.

## 14

A gathered at the Midville Park band shell, watching the end of the black-and-white movie *Tarzan the Ape Man* on the big screen.

Fake palm trees wave in the light of the full moon. The Midville electric model elephant, donated by a former mayor, a crazy Tarzan fan, nods its head and flaps its ears.

This all looks a little odd sitting next to the Fall Festival display of hay bales, pitchforks, funny-shaped gourds, torches, and pumpkins. But this is movie night. And, as always, it's free.

On-screen, Tarzan swings through the jungle on a vine.

Cheeta the chimpanzee grabs another vine and swings after him.

A small robot in the very back row of the band shell beeps quietly. "This makes no sense. Why is the human acting like an ape?"

"He's Tarzan," whispers Watson. "He was raised by apes."

Klank's antenna blinks in amazement. **"So he has decided that he is most happy when he is swinging through the jungle with his ape friends? That is nice."**

"That is not true," beeps Klink. "Humans do not live in trees."

"I would love to live in a tree and study monkeys and

apes all the time," says Janegoodall. "And someday I will."

"OK," says Frank, "get ready. As soon as the movie ends, we jump onstage and give our Electro-Finger demonstration, just as we planned."

Tarzan lands on a broad branch. He looks out over the tops of the jungle trees, cups his hands to his mouth, and—

The screen goes black.

The model elephant stops its electronic nodding and flapping.

The electric lights blink off, leaving the park lit only by moonlight.

"Hey!"

"What happened?"

"Check the power!"

But before the crowd completely freaks out, a small figure in an old-fashioned suit and a bad haircut walks to the middle of the stage, lit by a circle of light from the candle he carries in front of him.

"Nothing to worry about, good people of Midville," says a familiar, creepy voice booming through a megaphone. "Just a friendly reminder from your power company that we all love electricity and we all need electricity."

The figure blows out the candle.

"Lights!" booms the creepy voice.

The band shell lights pop back on and illuminate the last person Frank and Watson want to see.

Watson makes a face and says the kid's name like he is spitting out a bad taste.

"Edison!"

## 15

**W**ATSON IS RIGHT.

It is Edison. He stands in the middle of the stage, smiling. "Isn't electricity wonderful? It gives us light. It gives us heat. It gives us . . ." Edison motions toward the screen.

Tarzan reappears on-screen. Hands cupped to his mouth, he yodels his long, loopy Tarzan yell. THE END scrolls up over the black-and-white jungle.

T. Edison smiles another crooked smile. "Wonderful. All of this brought to you by your friendly local power company. You are welcome, Midville."

No one in the audience says thank you.

"It would be more wonderful if we didn't have to pay such crazy prices," calls Charlie the postman.

"We are working on energy prices every day," says T. Edison, not exactly lying about what he and Mr. Chimp have been doing, but not exactly telling the truth, either.

"Hogwash!" yells Fireman Chad.

"We're building our future," says T. Edison, pointing to a banner that has somehow just appeared between two palm trees. Edison adds, "If we knew a cheaper way to produce electricity, we certainly would."

This gives Frank Einstein a genius idea.

Frank weaves through the crowd, drags Watson up on-stage with him, and announces, "And that is exactly what we have come to show you—a better, cheaper way to produce electricity."

T. Edison is completely surprised but tries to act like he isn't. "Heckle and Jeckle, what are you doing here?"

"We should ask you the same thing," says Watson.

"I asked first."

The crowd starts rumbling, getting restless.

Frank unlatches his saxophone case and turns to the crowd. "Midville! I have just the invention that can help us all."

"A giant battery?" asks Ms. Priscilla, principal of Midville Academy.

"A new generator?" guesses Mr. Hacey, owner of the Give Me Pie! shop.

"Something even better," says Frank Einstein. "My lab partners and I—"

"Oh, for goodness' sake," fumes Edison. "Stop blabbering on. This is my event, you know."

"—we have used Nikola Tesla's idea of harnessing the electromagnetic energy of the Earth—which is everywhere—to produce and deliver wireless electricity."

"That is crazy," says Edison. "And dangerous."

"Not at all," answers Frank. "Allow me to demonstrate. Watson?"

Watson pulls three balloons out of his pocket. He blows up one balloon, rubs it on his hair, and leaves it sticking to his head. He blows up another balloon, rubs it, and sticks it. He blows up the last balloon, rubs it, and stands with all three balloons sticking to his head.

The crowd laughs.

"Ladies and gentleman," Frank announces, "electricity. Safe, wireless, and free."

"That is stupid," mutters Edison.

"But how can that help us?" Ms. Priscilla politely asks.

Frank smiles. "I have used the same idea of moving electrons"—Frank opens the saxophone case and fits his hand into the device tucked inside—"to make my newest invention . . ."

Frank raises his right hand, wearing a big metal glove with lights, buttons, an antenna, and one extended finger.

". . . the Electro-Finger!"

"Whoa," says Mr. Hacey.

"Oh my," says Ms. Priscilla.

"Cool," says Postman Charlie. "How does it work?"

Frank points the Electro-Finger at Watson.

Watson knocks the balloons off his head and pulls out a giant lightbulb.

"I will now use the Electro-Finger to gather magnetic energy from the Earth, change it to electricity, and deliver it wirelessly to light the bulb in Watson's hand!"

"This is completely stupid and completely dangerous," Edison announces to the crowd. "Do not believe this Frank Einstein garbage."

"Ready, Watson?"

Watson holds the lightbulb out, suddenly having second thoughts about the electrical energy coming his way. What if Edison is right?

Frank answers for Watson. "Ready!"

He pushes the button at the base of the glove. The tip glows.

"Electro-Finger! Transmitting electricity . . ."

Frank pushes a second button.

". . . now!"

Watson believes the Electro-Finger will safely transmit electricity, but he closes his eyes just in case and holds the bulb as far away from himself as possible.

The thin wire filament inside the lightbulb glows a faint orange. It pulses. It flickers. It suddenly shines a brilliant white.

"Beautiful," says Ms. Priscilla.

Watson opens his eyes and starts breathing again.

"Energy," says Frank.

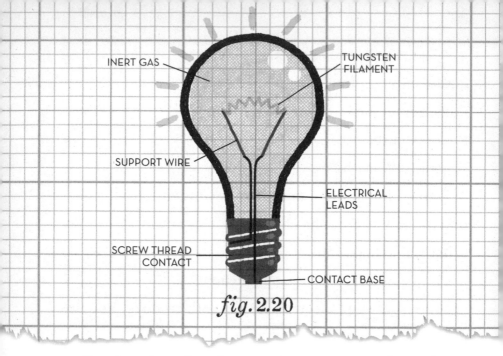

INERT GAS

TUNGSTEN FILAMENT

SUPPORT WIRE

ELECTRICAL LEADS

SCREW THREAD CONTACT

CONTACT BASE

*fig.* **2.20**

Frank points the Electro-Finger at an unplugged row of lights.

"Wireless!"

The lights flash on.

Frank's Electro-Finger zaps the projector.

"Safe!"

The film restarts, and Tarzan yodels his Tarzan yell.

Frank waves the Electro-Finger. "And free for everyone!"

"Hooray for Frank Einstein!" Janegoodall starts cheering from the back.

The Midville Park free-movie crowd copies Jane-goodall and begins cheering and clapping.

Frank Einstein holds up his genius invention and smiles.

But T. Edison does not cheer.

T. Edison looks at the electric model elephant and hatches his own genius plan.

16

T. Edison tries to smile, but it looks like it is hurting his face. He peeks backstage. While no one is looking, he signs instructions to Mr. Chimp, who is hidden in the shadows.

Mr. Chimp nods and gets to work, fiddling with something inside the electric elephant.

"Very impressive," Edison's voice booms through the movie speakers, drowning out the clapping and the cheering. "But I am still very concerned about safety."

"You saw it for yourself. It works safely," says Watson.

Edison nods. He checks to see Mr. Chimp crossing two

particular wires, with no one noticing him, and signing back:

O    K

Now T. Edison smiles for real. "Yes, yes. Your Finger Thing lit one lightbulb. But what if it had to do more work? With more electricity? Wouldn't it be *more* dangerous?"

"Not at all," says Frank.

"Well," says Edison, "if you're so sure, it shouldn't be a problem for you to power dear Topsy, our beloved Midville elephant."

Frank and Watson exchange a glance. They both wonder what Edison might be up to.

"Give it the Electro-Finger!" yells Charlie the postman.

"Yeah, do that!" adds Fireman Chad.

"OK," says Frank Einstein. "That should be simple enough."

Frank sets the Electro-Finger on LOW, aims it at the model elephant, and presses the button.

Slowly the elephant begins to raise its trunk.

Frank increases the power. The elephant shakes its head and flaps its ears. Watson nods and smiles.

In the shadows, Klank bangs his monkey-wrench hand on the side of his metal body as Frank gives Topsy full Electro-Finger power.

The mechanical elephant raises its trunk and trumpets.

Janegoodall starts the crowd clapping and cheering again.

And that is when a faint wisp of smoke starts leaking out Topsy's left ear.

Edison points at the smoke so the crowd doesn't miss it. "Oh no!" Edison calls, in fake alarm.

Frank quickly shuts down the Electro-Finger. But Topsy smokes out both ears now. She twitches. She shakes.

"Make it stop!" someone in the crowd yells.

Frank holds up the Electro-Finger to show that it's off, but no one sees. All eyes are on Topsy.

The elephant shakes and shudders. She smokes and

convulses. In one last burst of smoke and a twitch, she tips over and falls with a resounding *THUD*.

"Einstein's Electro-Finger electrocuted Topsy!" someone screams.

"That invention is a death machine!"

"Oh my!"

"AIEEEEEEEEEEEE!"

Someone throws a Fall Festival gourd, and it splatters wetly onstage.

Klank grabs Klink and from out of the shadows jumps to protect Frank and Watson. **"Frank Einstein is good! The Electro-Finger is a good invention! I will give you all hugs!"** Klank extends his flexible metal arms.

"Oh no," says Watson, more to himself than to anyone else. "That does not look good."

"Killer robots, too?!" another hysterical voice screams.

A small orange pumpkin bounces off Klank and splits in half, dripping its stringy pumpkin guts.

"Frank Einstein is creating monsters!" yells someone who sounds exactly like T. Edison trying to disguise his voice.

"No, wait—" Frank starts to explain.

But then the crowd starts taking apart the rest of the Fall Festival display and moving toward the stage.

Janegoodall understands the dangerous power of the crowd mind. She runs toward the backstage exit and calls out to her friends, "Follow me, NOW!"

Frank, Watson, Klink, and Klank follow Janegoodall.

The crowd of angry Midville villagers swarms after them, shaking pitchforks and lifting burning torches, calling, "Frank Einstein is creating monsters!"

## 17

F **LUFFY WHITE CLOUDS DRIFT ACROSS THE BRIGHT BLUE SKY OVER** Grampa Al's Fix It! shop. Rays of morning sunlight **(A)** beam down to the repaired roof, onto a dark blue panel angled toward the rising sun.

The energy from the sunlight is absorbed by the solar panel **(B)**.

The sunlight-energized material of the solar panel frees charged electrons **(C)**.

The charged electrons flow as direct current through the wire **(D)**.

The current travels down through the roof to the power inverter **(E)**, which changes the direct current into alternating current.

The alternating current snakes through the main electric line **(F)**.

Around Frank's bedroom **(G)**.

Into Grampa Al's kitchen **(H)**.

Behind the atomic clock **(I)**.

Out of the wall outlet next to the refrigerator **(J)**.

Through the power cord and into the toaster **(K)**.

Around the toaster coils, heating them orange-hot.

Browning the bread in the slots and making—

*Ding!*

"Toast," says Grampa Al. "One of the true wonders of the world. Don't you think so, boys?"

Frank holds his head in his hands. He doesn't say anything.

Watson, who has slept over, looks just as shell-shocked.

Grampa Al cracks one last egg into the bowl and stirs. "How can you guys not love toast? Who doesn't love toast?" he says, holding the slice of bread up to the light.

Frank and Watson don't move.

Grampa Al notices. "It's a beautiful new day. Why the long face, Einstein?"

Frank holds up his Electro-Finger. "They called Klink

and Klank monsters. They think my invention fried Topsy."

"Edison and his creepy monkey did it!" says Watson. "I don't know how they did. But I'm sure it was them!"

"Ape," Frank corrects Watson.

Grampa Al pours the beaten eggs into butter sizzling in the pan. "Well, you know what I always used to say when I was working as a chef . . ."

"What?" says Frank. "You never told me you were a chef."

"You never asked," says Grampa Al. "But I always said, 'You can't make an omelet without breaking some eggs.'"

Grampa Al flips the eggs in the pan into a perfect half circle.

"*You* made up that saying?" marvels Frank.

"What does that even mean?" asks Watson.

"**The ingredients for an omelet are eggs,**" Klink explains. "**So eggs must be broken to be made into an omelet.**"

Grampa Al flips the omelet in the pan, slices it in half, and slides one half onto Frank's plate and the other half onto Watson's. "It means that to make something good, you sometimes have to wreck something else."

Klank beeps. "**Yes. Exactly. Like, why did the sim–**

ple machine throw the clock out the window?"

"Oh no. Please do not start this again," says Klink.

"Why?" asks Grampa Al.

"It wanted to see time fly. Ha-ha-ha." Klank's antenna flashes blue and green. "And why did the simple machine put his clock inside a safe?"

"No, no, no . . ." begs Klink. "Your bad jokes crash my system!"

Grampa Al can't help himself. "Why?" he asks.

"It wanted to save time. Ha-ha-ha."

*Flash flash flash.* Klink spins in a circle, his GPS hiccuping, "Recalculating. Recalculating." His brain software crashes with a small *ding.*

Grampa Al sits down next to Frank. "But the saying that is probably more to the point here is: Beware of snakes in the grass."

"Right!" says Watson, now hungrily digging into his omelet. "Uh . . . why?"

"Watch out for dangers you can't see," says Grampa Al. "History is full of scientists whose ideas were frightening or odd at first . . . but were then made popular by other people, who took credit for the work. Your guy Nikola Tesla is a great example. Not everyone knows his name ... or how important his work was in perfecting radio, television, wireless, even the alternating-current electricity that everyone uses today. The electricity we used to toast this toast. All brought to us by Tesla's work."

"Or like the guy who invented potato chips!" adds Watson. "One of my favorite inventions of all time! But who knows his name?"

Klink boots back to life. He reports, "George Crum. A cook at a restaurant in Saratoga Springs, New York, in 1853. He sliced potatoes as thin as he could and fried them to satisfy a fussy customer."

Frank Einstein absentmindedly scratches his head with the tip of the Electro-Finger. "So we have to watch out for Edison. And figure out how to show people that our invention really is something good."

"But how do we do that?" asks Watson, finally picking up his toast.

"The Midville Police Station might be a good place to start," answers Grampa Al.

**"Please do not put us in jail!"** bleeps Klank.

"My pal Police Chief Jacobs just might need your help," says Grampa Al, finishing his perfect toast. "I saw him this morning at Poetry Club, and it sounds like he's got his hands full with all kinds of power-plant troubles."

Frank Einstein gulps down the last of his omelet and nods. "If we can help Chief Jacobs, everyone will know the Electro-Finger is good."

"Poetry Club?" asks Watson.

"You never asked," answers Grampa Al with a big smile.

## 18

FLUFFY WHITE CLOUDS DRIFT ACROSS THE BRIGHT BLUE SKY OVER the field in the middle of the Midville Woods. Rays of morning sunlight beam down to the trees, the grass field, the hundreds of dark blue panels angled toward the sun.

These panels are the Midville Solar Array.

The energy from the sunlight is absorbed by the hundreds of panels covering the field. This sunlight energy frees electrons in the layers of solar-panel material. And these free electrons then flow as electricity.

A pair of bright orange-and-black monarch butterflies flap over the sea of solar panels. A red-breasted robin

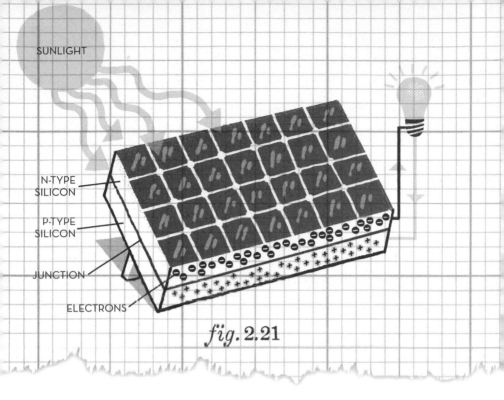

SUNLIGHT

N-TYPE
SILICON

P-TYPE
SILICON

JUNCTION

ELECTRONS

*fig.* 2.21

sweetly tweets. A curious chipmunk pops his head out of his hole and sits, looking oh so cute, until—

*WHAAAAAAAMMMM! WHAAAAAAAAMMMM! WHAAAAAAAMMMM!*

The solar panels, metal supports, robin, and curious chipmunk are smashed in an explosion of broken solar-panel bits and pieces. The butterflies are blown away by a blast of black engine exhaust.

*WHAAAAAAAAMMMM! WHAAAAAAAAMMMM! WHAAAAAAAMMMM!*

Enormous spiked-metal feet shatter panel after panel after panel with their stomping steps.

A flock of crows escapes to the trees, panicked and cawing the whole way.

More freaked-out chipmunks, terrified field mice, and one slow groundhog dive to safety underground.

*WHAAAAAAAMMMM! WHAAAAAAAMMMM! WHAAAAAAMMMM!*

The giant feet *clomp-stomp-smash-shatter* their way up one solar row, and *blam-stamp-bust* down another.

*WHAAAAAAAMMMM! WHAAAAAAAMMMM! WHAAAAAAMMMM!*

The giant feet are attached to thick mechanical legs. The legs are powered by a squat motor body. A glass cab sits atop the motor body. And in the glass cab of this custom-built Bigfoot Stomper machine, a chimpanzee push-pulls the two hand levers back and forth, back and forth, raising and lowering the monster metal feet.

Edison, wearing his orange safety helmet, yells over the noise of the Bigfoot engine and the shattering solar panels.

"Beautiful! Just beautiful!"

Mr. Chimp pauses, pulls, holds the huge right foot over the last solar panel. He signs:

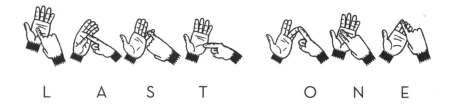

L A S T     O N E

And pushes the lever to drop the steel foot and smash the last panel into broken junk.

T. Edison pulls out his notebook and makes one last big check in it.

Fluffy white clouds still drift across the bright blue sky.

Rays of sunlight still beam down to the grassy field.

But there are no solar panels left.

Nothing to gather the energy of the sun.

Nothing to convert sunlight to electricity.

any townspeople, hiding the Electro-Finger in a plain backpack.

Klank follows right behind, propelling himself with semi-controlled bursts of his foot-jets, holding Klink and trying his best to look like some kind of completely not-dangerous-to-anyone motorized vehicle.

Frank and Watson park their bikes in the lot behind the Midville Police Department, and all four hustle in the back door. They hear Police Chief Jacobs before they see him.

"Ten-four! Unit One, report latest on the Midville Coal Plant!"

*BZZZZT BZZZZT.*

"Ten-four! Unit Two, report latest on the Midville Wind Farm!"

*BZZZZZT BZZZZT.*

"Well, find something! These power plants aren't wrecking themselves!"

Frank and Watson step into police headquarters and see Chief Jacobs hunched over an old-fashioned microphone, directing police-radio traffic.

"Oh, hey, guys," he says, and waves Frank and Watson over to an old green leather couch. "Take a load off. This day has started crazier than a fruitcake and busier than a cat in a full litter box!"

Frank laughs. He remembers why Chief Jacobs and Grampa Al are such good friends.

Klank peeks around the corner.

*BZZZZZT BZZZZZT.*

"Yep . . . uh-huh . . . right . . . ten-four," Chief

Jacobs says into the microphone. "And tell Klink and Klank to come in and make themselves comfortable. Or at least robot comfortable."

"What?" says Frank.

"How did you know about Klink and Klank?" asks Watson.

*BZZZZZT BZZZZT.*

"Poetry Club. Your grampa and I talk."

Klink rolls in and sits on the couch. Klank plops down next to him.

"Frank Einstein and his merry band," says Chief Jacobs. "What can I do you boys for?"

**"Huh?"** says Klank.

"We might be able to help you, Chief," says Frank. "And you might be able to help us prove to the people of Midville that my invention"—Frank pulls the Electro-Finger out of his backpack—"is not dangerous."

Chief Jacobs leans back in his swivel chair. "I heard all about the unfortunate elephant incident last night."

"That wasn't the Electro-Finger's fault!" says Watson.

"But everyone thinks it was," says the chief. "I wish there was something I could do . . . some way you could show that the Electro-Finger does good, not harm. But I just don't—"

*BZZZZT BZZZZZT.*

The speaker squawks, "Ten sixty-seven, Chief! Ten sixty-seven! Caller says Midville Solar Array is being attacked by some kind of robot monster. Repeat—Midville Solar Array being attacked by a robot monster."

Chief Jacobs jumps up. "Unit Three to the Midville Solar Array," he barks into his radio. "Unit Three to the Solar Array. Right now!"

The radio beeps. "Um, we don't have a Unit Three, Chief. We only have two."

Chief Jacobs yells at his radio. "Aw, dang it, Sergeant Susan! What are we supposed to do now?"

Frank Einstein jumps off the couch. "We are on it, Chief!"

"Great idea, Einstein!" says Chief Jacobs.

Frank leads the charge out the back door. "Come on, guys. Electro-Finger to the Solar Array's rescue!"

## 20

**F**dirt path. They skid around boulders and jump small logs, hustling to the Midville Solar Array as fast as they can.

Klank runs a clomping, crashing, straight line behind them, but instead of using the path, he stomps right through the brush and over small trees—carrying (and wildly swinging) Klink by his handy Shop-Vac handle.

"How embarrassing," says Klink. "I simply must make myself a more dignified form of transportation."

**"BAM BAM BAM!"** answers Klank, smashing happily along.

Frank, Watson, Klink, and Klank burst out of the woods and into the open meadow. The tall grass waves in the wind.

All four stop dead in their tracks at the sight in front of them. What used to be neat rows of blue solar panels angled toward the sun . . . is now a graveyard heap of broken glass and silicon bits, twisted metal supports, and snapped wires.

"We have to find out who this helps," says Watson. "We have to follow the energy."

A crazy scream of crushed metal and a deep, diesel-motor roar answers. It's a huge metal beast with massive spiked feet, stomping the wreckage of the Solar Array to even smaller pieces.

Klank screams, **"Robot monster!"** and drops Klink in the weeds.

Frank jumps off his bike, whips the Electro-Finger out of his backpack, and straps it on. "We have to stop this thing now!" he yells over the shrieking and pounding. "Watson, you go left. Klink and Klank, go right. When it chases you, I'll Electro-Finger-zap it."

Watson hops off his bike. "Wait, what? You're using us as bait?"

The metal monster stomps some glass and heads right toward the guys.

"Yes," says Frank Einstein, with calculated cool. "Now go!"

Klank grabs Klink. **"Attack the robot monster!"**

"Stooooop swiiiiiinginggggg meeeeeeee!"

Klank runs right. The monster giant-steps right.

Watson runs left. The metal beast giant-steps left.

Frank kneels to steady his arm on one knee. He dials the Electro-Finger to MAX.

The metal monster lifts a spiked foot right over Watson.

"Aieeeeeee!" yells a running Watson. "Now, now, now, Einstein!"

Frank takes careful aim and fires an electromagnetic

burst of energy toward what he hopes is the heart of the monster.

Watson jumps for the tall grass over the hill, screaming, "*Eeeeeeeeeeeeeee!*"

The thing lunges, belches a smoke-billowing roar . . . then—*screeeeeech, creak*—freezes on one leg and falls over sideways, landing with a huge, metal *THWUMMMP!*

Frank lowers the Electro-Finger and cautiously approaches the felled monster. Klank appears from behind a bush and carries Klink over.

**"Is the robot monster dead?"** asks Klank.

"It was never alive," says Klink. "It is a machine."

Frank inspects the hulk. "A very amazing custom demolition machine . . ."

Klank takes a step closer. The side of the thing's skull suddenly swings open.

**"Shoot it!"** yells Klank. **"Zap it again!"**

Frank lifts the Electro-Finger. But before he can fire, a familiar kid

with a bad haircut pops out of the machine and jumps to the ground. He stands with his hands on his hips, and he is not happy.

"Oh, great! It's genius Frank Einstein, his genius Dum-Bots, and his dangerous Killer-Finger again."

"Edison?"

"More genius," says Edison.

A chimpanzee in dress pants and a hard hat hops out of the machine. He flips open the engine panel, runs a quick check, and turns to yell at Frank, *"Eeeee-eeee-eee oooo-oooo!"*

"You have made Mr. Chimp very mad. This is his Bigfoot Stomper machine. And you fried its electronics."

Frank lowers the Electro-Finger. "But it . . . You were destroying the Midville Solar Array. You can't do that."

Mr. Chimp narrows his eyes, stares at Frank, and disappears around the back of the Bigfoot Stomper machine.

Edison leans against the metal hulk and smiles. "And that's where you're completely wrong, genius Einstein. I can do whatever I want with the Midville Solar Array. Because I own it."

Edison points to a giant banner hanging over the Midville Solar Array sign.

Klank slowly reads, **"'Building Our Future.'"**

"Very good reading, DumBot." Edison turns back to look at the landscape of smashed solar panels. "Now get off my property before I have you arrested. Or worse."

Frank looks at Edison. "So that's what you are up to, you snake in the grass. Destroying all the other sources of energy . . . and making mine look bad. Let's get out of here, guys."

Frank, Klink, and Klank head for the bikes.

"Watson!" calls Frank. No answer.

**"Watson!"** booms Klank. Still no answer.

Frank, Klink, and Klank search the whole smashed Solar Array. No Watson.

"Get out of here!" yells Edison. "Now!"

But Watson has disappeared.

And, suspiciously enough, so has Mr. Chimp.

## 21

K for Watson.

Watson is not at the lab. He is not at his house.

Frank searches north. Klink searches east. Klank searches west.

Watson is not at the library, the park, the candy store, the diner, the baseball diamond, the oak tree above town. No Watson uptown, downtown, east side, west side. No Watson anywhere.

Frank, Klink, and Klank meet back at the lab. They sit down at the workbench, and Frank rolls out a map of Midville that they study, puzzling over where Watson could be.

"If Watson had a GPS signal like I do," says Klink, "I could track him on my map."

**"If Watson could sing robot songs like I do,"** says Klank, **"I could find him with my song locator."**

"He doesn't have a GPS, and he can't sing at all," says Frank. "But if I know Watson, he's trying to solve this mystery."

**"What mystery?"** beeps Klank.

"The mystery of why Edison is buying up energy-supply companies . . . and wrecking them." Frank scratches his head. "What was the last thing Watson said?"

Klink checks his robot memory. He replays Watson's *"Eeeeeeeeeeeeeee!"*

"No," says Frank. "Before that. The thing he said about tracking something down."

Klink searches his records. He plays: *"We have to find out who this helps. We have to follow the energy."*

"That's it!" says Frank. "That's our answer to where Watson is. He followed the energy. To the one energy source still working."

**"The robot monster's house?"** asks Klank.

Frank Einstein mentally checks off the destroyed power sources:

—the Midville Coal Plant

—the Midville Wind Farm

—the Midville Solar Array

Grampa Al sticks his head in Frank's lab to complain about losing all electricity. "That darn Midville Power and Light company!"

"Exactly," says Frank.

**"Huh?"** says Klank.

Twenty minutes later, at the shoreline of the lake just above the only power-supply source in Midville still working—the Midville Hydroelectric Dam—Frank Einstein is, once again, proved right.

**"Watson!"** booms Klank. He gives Watson, who happens to be tied and taped to the front of an inflatable raft, a giant Klank hug.

"Watson!" beeps Klink from the bottom of the raft, where Klank has dropped him.

"Exactly," says Frank, hopping into the raft to untape him. "Watson."

Everyone is so excited that no one notices a long, dark, not-human hand untie the raft, push it gently out into the water flowing toward the dam, and sign:

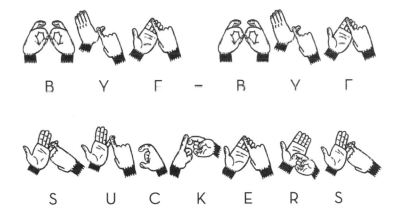

B Y E - B Y E

S U C K E R S

## 22

NERGY," SAYS FRANK EINSTEIN, KID GENIUS AND INVENTOR.

E "NERGY," SAYS FRANK EINSTEIN, KID GENIUS AND INVENTOR. "Power that can be converted into motion, light, heat—energy in all its different forms! That's what this is all about, Watson."

"MMMmphh mmm rrrmmm mmm," answers Watson.

Frank nods. "Oh yes. Of course—also forces. The way energy is applied. The way energy works in the world. Absolutely right, Watson."

Watson wiggles. "Rrrrarr rrrr ruuhhhh ruhhhh!"

Frank Einstein scratches his head with an oversized metal finger. "Oh yeah! This is the perfect chance to test my **HYPOTHESIS** . . . and the ultimate challenge for my Electro-Finger invention."

Watson, lashed to the front of a rubber raft drifting ever faster toward a roaring sound at the base of the dam in the river, would like to say, "Einstein, this is it! I'm done! You're crazy. This is *not* the perfect chance to test *anything*! And: HELLLLLLLP!"

But Watson can't say any of that.

Because Watson is not only taped to the raft.

His mouth is also duct-taped completely shut.

So all he can do is wiggle, bug his eyes out, and make noises.

"We are presently moving quickly toward a column of water being sucked under the dam," says Klink.

"Uh-oh," says Klank.

"Good OBSERVATION," says Frank.

The sucking sound of the dark, whirlpooling water ahead grows suddenly louder and scarier.

Watson shakes his head and "MMMrrr rrrr rrrrrs" some more.

"I've seen a diagram of this plant," says Frank. "That whirlpool is caused by the intake under the dam. The water spins a monster-size turbine . . . which runs the generator . . . which spins metal wire inside a magnetic field . . . which then produces electricity."

"Quite right," confirms Klink.

**"I do not want to get sucked underwater and chopped into little bits by a monster turbine!"**

"RRRRaaa reeeee reee!" adds Watson.

Frank crouches in the front of the raft, resting the Electro-Finger on Watson's stomach to aim it. "So! My hypothesis is—if I can hit the generator with a charge of electricity from the Electro-Finger . . . it will shock-stop the generator. The stopped generator will freeze the turbine. The water intake will stop. And we will be free."

The raft draws closer to the whirlpool.

Now the deep, powerful hum of the spinning turbine rumbles scary-loud.

"Hmmm," says Klink.

**"Ooooooooh,"** says Klank, hugging the sides of the raft.

"Eeeeeeee," moans Watson, thrashing and bugging his eyes out.

"Great!" says Frank. "I knew you guys would approve. Begin **EXPERIMENT!**"

Frank points the Electro-Finger down into the whirlpool, where the base of the dam should be.

"This burst of electrons should hit the generator, reverse its north and south magnetic poles, and stop the generator . . ."

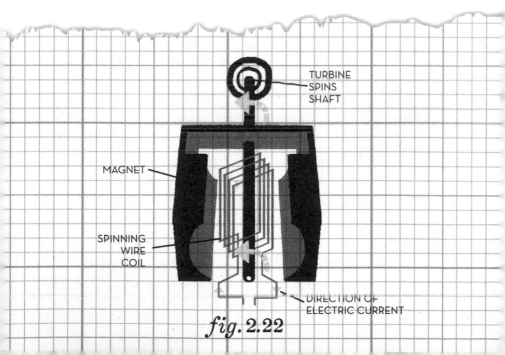

TURBINE
SPINS
SHAFT

MAGNET

SPINNING
WIRE
COIL

DIRECTION OF
ELECTRIC CURRENT

*fig.* **2.22**

Watson nods.

" . . . which should stop the turbine from spinning . . ."

Watson nods nods nods.

" . . . which should keep us from getting sucked under-
water and chopped to bits."

The raft spins around the outer ring of the whirlpool.

"Quite possibly," says Klink.

**"I do not like water,"** says Klank.

"RRR-rrreeee!" urges Watson.

Frank aims into the whirlpool where he guesses the
generator is located. He pulls the Electro-Finger's trigger.

The lights on the dam pop on . . . and off . . . and on again.

The raft spins farther into the circling whirlpool, picking up speed, drifting deeper into the sucking hole in the
lake.

Frank lowers his aim and fires again.

The lights on the dam strobe more quickly.

Then pop.

The whirlpool swirls, unchanged.

"Hmmm," says Frank, examining the end of the
Electro-Finger.

Now Watson and Frank can clearly hear the deep thrum

of the turbine blades chopping through the dark, cold water far below them. The raft slips into the funnel and below the flat surface of the lake.

"That doesn't seem to have worked the way I thought it would . . ."

"Hrrrrrrrr!" says Watson.

"What?" asks Frank.

"IIRRRRRRR!!!"

Frank leans forward and pulls the tape off Watson's mouth.

"What?"

"HELLLLLLLLLLLLLLLLLLLLLLLLLLLLLLLLLLLLLL
LLLLLLLLLLLLLLLLLLLLLLLLLLLLLLLLLLLLLLLL
LLLLLLLLLLLLLLLLLLLLLLLLLLLLLLLLLLLLLLLL
LLLLLLLLLLLLLLLLLLLLLLLLLLLLLLLLLLLLLLLL
LLLLLLLLLLLLLLLLLLLLLLLLLLLLLLLLLLLLLLLL
LLLLLLLLLLLLLLLLLLLLLLLLLLLLLLLLLLLLLLLL
LLLLLLLLLLLLLLLLLLLLLLLLLLLLLLLLLLLLLLLL
LLLLLLLLLLLLLLLLLLLLLLLLLLLLLLLLLLLLLLLL
LLLLLLLLLLLLLLLLLLLLLLLLLLLLLLLLLLLLLLLL
LLLLLLLLLLLLLLLLLLLLLLLLLLLLLLLLLLLLLLLL
LLLLLLLLLLLLLLLLLLLLLLLLLLLLLLLLLLLLLLLLLLL

## 23

thirty-two meters above ground level, on a tall hill, in the operator's cab of a tower crane, through the lenses of black, compact, folding, day- and night-vision binoculars, T. Edison watches a small raft spin around a whirlpool next to the Midville Hydro-electric Dam.

T. Edison watches the raft drop into the swirling funnel and disappear from view.

"Success! What a fantastic plan!"

Mr. Chimp, still wearing his yellow hard hat, gives a thumbs-up and turns back to the crane controls.

"We are nowhere near Lake Midville. That lamebrain Einstein and his dorky friend and idiot robots have just had a terrible hydroelectric-turbine accident. It's clear I had nothing to do with it, because I am miles away. And everyone will forget about Einstein's stupid 'free wireless energy' invention."

Mr. Chimp pulls the cab control joystick toward himself with one big toe. The cab glides down the tower back toward the ground.

"Now *all* of Midville must buy its power from *me!*"

Mr. Chimp's big toe twitches forward.

The cab jerks to a stop, still twenty meters above the ground.

Edison lurches up, then falls back into his seat. "I wish you would learn how to operate your heavy machinery just a bit more smoothly."

Mr. Chimp stares at Edison.

"What?"

Mr. Chimp stares.

A red-tailed hawk flies by at cab-window level.

"What?"

Mr. Chimp signs:

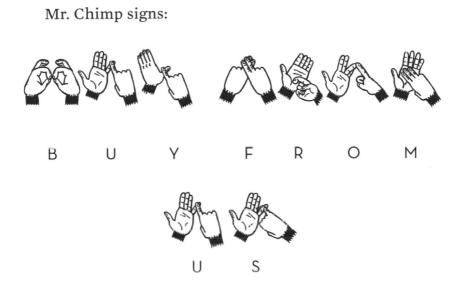

B    U    Y    F    R    O    M

U    S

Edison frowns. "Listen, you tree-swinging reject. Edison Energy is *my* company, and people will be buying energy from *me,* not *us.* Edison Energy. Not Chimp Energy. You will get your share. Now stop monkeying around . . . and get us down on the ground so I can get to the real work."

Mr. Chimp takes his feet off the controls.

He leans forward until his chimp nose is almost touching Edison's human nose. Mr. Chimp tenses the muscles in his face, pulling his lips up and slightly apart.

It looks like a smile. But it is not a smile.

Mr. Chimp leans back in his seat. He pulls his operator's seat belt tight, pauses for two seconds, then jams the control joystick UP, DOWN, TILT LEFT, TILT RIGHT . . .

Edison slides-flips-flops out of his seat, smacks against the cab's glass side, and sees the ground twenty long meters below.

Mr. Chimp toggles DOWN, TILT, DROP, TILT, UP, FREE FALL.

"I was just kidding!" yells Edison. He bounces off the ceiling, then the floor.

"Stop!"

*Smack, bang, boom.*

Mr. Chimp pauses.

"OK, OK. It's *our* company—EdisonChimp."

Mr. Chimp reaches for the control joystick again.

"*OK!* ChimpEdison!"

Mr. Chimp leans back again. He nods. He folds his arms behind his head, grips the joystick with his left toe, and eases the cab smoothly to the ground.

Edison crawls back into his seat, now with a lump on his forehead. He turns to look out the glass wall and mumbles something that sounds an awful lot like "Dumb monkey."

Mr. Chimp hears. He doesn't care about insults. But he does care about accuracy. He signs:

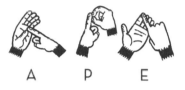

A    P    E

Then he twitches two muscles in his face.
And this time he smiles a real smile.

LLLLLLLL LLLLLLLLLLLLLLLLLLLLLLLLLP!"

**F**RANK PUTS THE TAPE BACK OVER WATSON'S MOUTH.

Frank quickly slides the lever up on the Electro-Finger. "Maybe just a bit more power." Frank aims the Electro-Finger down into the whirlpool and pulls the trigger.

Klink's webcam eye twirls in circles. "Beeeeeeeeeep."

"Oops. Sorry, Klink." Frank adjusts the frequency knob and pulls the Electro-Finger trigger again.

Klank's antenna blinks off and on. His keyboard starts playing "Old MacDonald Had a Farm."

"Sorry, sorry, sorry."

The raft spirals deeper into the whirlpool.

Frank looks up, analyzing the situation. "Well, so much for *that* hypothesis."

Watson wriggles out of his ropes and rips the tape off his mouth. "*Hypothesis?* I've got a hypothesis! We are goners!"

Franks powers down the Electro-Finger.

Klink's eye stops spinning. Klank's antenna stops flashing. "Old MacDonald" grinds to a stop.

"That's not really a hypothesis," says Frank. "It's more an observation. Maybe even an opinion."

"Aieeeeee!" says Watson. "What if we jump? Maybe we can swim out of this."

The raft spins crazily around the inside of the whirlpool.

"OK!" says Frank. "Now *that's* a hypothesis. But not a very good one. We can't overpower the water."

"We have to do something!" says Watson.

"Electrical energy didn't work," says Frank, thinking out loud. "Maybe some other form of energy would."

**"Sound energy!"** bleeps Klank. **"Badang badang badang."**

Klank blasts his Robot Boogie. **"Badang badang badang."**

The raft circles faster. The turbine hum vibrates louder.

Frank shakes his head. "No."

Klink holds up his magnet attachment and corkscrew.

"No, and no," mutters Frank.

Watson desperately searches his pockets. "My peashooter!"

"Hmmm . . ." Frank scratches his head. "Yes, Watson. That's it!"

The nose of the raft tilts down, headed for the humming, thrashing bottom.

Watson loads his peashooter, trusting that Frank Einstein has a genius idea. "Who do I shoot? What? Where?"

"No shooting!" Frank yells over the growing roar of the sloshing water and the churning turbine. "But let's use the same principle! Newton's Third Law!"

"For every action there is an equal and opposite reaction," Klink quotes calmly.

"*Yes!*" says Frank. "Klank! Set your rockets on FULL THRUST and stick your feet out the back of the raft!"

The raft twists and shudders. Watson grabs the front of it to keep from falling over.

Klank uses his monkey-wrench hand to turn his rockets

to FULL THRUST. **"I knew my new hand would come in handy!"** Klank obeys Frank's command and sticks his feet out the back of the raft.

"Everyone hang on tight! Klank, fire your rockets!"

Klank pushes the green button on his side, and his mini Saturn V F-1 foot rockets ignite with a small *ffwump*.

The raft circles the inside of the whirlpool more quickly. But now it rises, slowly spiraling up the tunnel of water. Frank Einstein yells, "More power!"

Klank increases his foot rockets to OVER THRUST.

The raft surges. Frank turns Klank to steer.

Klink observes the wall of water rushing by. "Too late."

"More power!" calls Frank.

With his monkey wrench, Klank twists his rockets to CRAZY THRUST. The jet blasts push the raft faster, faster, around, around, around . . . and suddenly back up to the lake's surface. The raft speeds toward shore.

"Hooray for Newton!" cheers Frank.

"Hooray for Klank!" cheers Watson.

"Very interesting application of force," muses Klink.

The guys laugh and smile . . . and then hear a terrible sound.

The sound of no sound coming from Klank's jets.

"Uh-oh," says Klank. "Ran out of rocket fuel."

The raft slows, stops, and begins to drift, spinning and powerless, back toward the turbine whirlpool.

G hard to keep up with Mr. Chimp.

Mr. Chimp raises one eyebrow.

"Today the town of Midville is ours. Tomorrow . . . the world."

Mr. Chimp powerfully and effortlessly pedals his custom chimp-size racing bike.

"We are about to be richer than anyone can imagine. I will build the biggest, best, most amazing laboratory in the world," says Edison. "How about you, Mr. Chimp? What will you do with your share of the money?"

Mr. Chimp glides downhill and thinks about that.

He rides no-handed and signs:

T I R E

S W I N G

"What?" says Edison. "That's it?"

Mr. Chimp stares at Edison.

He adds:

F R E E D O M

T. Edison doesn't know what to think of that. It doesn't make any sense to him. So he just ignores it.

T. Edison and Mr. Chimp wheel into the Edison estate, under the stone entrance arch, down the driveway lined with sugar maple trees, and up to the grand Edison mansion.

They drop their bikes on the perfectly trimmed front lawn and walk through the massive oak double doors.

"Oh, there you are, sweetie," says Edison's mother.

"Please don't call me that in front of my workers, Mom."

"Call you what?"

"That thing you said."

"What did I say, sweetie?"

"That," says Edison out of the side of his mouth. "Don't call me 'sweetie.' My workers won't respect me."

"Oh, no one cares that I call you 'sweetie,'" says Mrs. Edison. "And this is not your worker. This is your Mr. Chimpy Wimpy."

"And *do not* call him that!"

"You named him."

"When I was two years old!"

"Oh, stop with all your fussing, sweetie."

Mr. Chimp laughs a panting little "Heh-heh-heh."

*"See?"* whines Edison.

"Well, never mind. I just wanted to tell you that the funny new red light on your desk has been blinking, and some kind of horn has been honking."

Edison's eyes open wide. "My Hydroelectric Turbine warning?"

"If that's what you call it . . ."

"That only triggers when the turbine stops!"

Mr. Chimp signs:

U    H    –    O    H

## 26

**K**LANK STANDS UP.

The raft picks up speed, drifts more quickly back toward certain hydroelectric-turbine-chopping disaster.

Klink makes thousands, millions, of almost-instant calculations and concludes, "Not good."

Frank and Watson desperately, unsuccessfully, try to paddle with their hands.

Klank fires up all 8K of his digital memory to connect exactly two thoughts. **"Must protect my humans. Every action has equal and opposite reaction. Yes, Frank Einstein?"**

Frank looks up. "Yes."

Klank nods.

Klank uses his monkey wrench to crank his Robot Boogie song up to LOUD. **BADANG BADANG BADANG.** He stands on the edge of the raft and yells, **"Action!"**

Klink starts to say, "I believe we have established that sound energy does not—"

And Klank suddenly dives off the front of the raft, straight into the whirlpool. The 214-pound force of his dive pushes the raft in an equal reaction—away from the whirlpool, all the way to shore.

Frank, Watson, and Klink jump to dry land. They look back just in time to see Klank's rocket-footed legs flip up and disappear, spinning down, down, down into the whirlpool.

The sound-wave beats of Klank's Robot Boogie echo through the water like a crazy whale song. Then, suddenly, inevitably, a horrible metal grinding-wrenching-screeching-chopping sound drowns out the Robot Boogie.

The deep bass hum of the turbine stops.

The whirlpool slows and disappears.

The surface of the lake falls into a quiet, perfectly level calm.

Frank, Watson, and Klink stand looking at the spot where Klank disappeared. They are safe. But they are stunned. Because they know, without looking, what they will find on the other side of the dam.

Nothing but crushed-up Klank parts.

## 27

**N**O! NO! NO!"

Edison pounds his desk with one small fist, yelling at the blinking red light above the label HYDROELECTRIC TURBINE.

"Do not tell me that dim-bulb Einstein and his idiot friends somehow wrecked my dam!"

Mr. Chimp examines the images on his computer monitor. He opens three new windows, scrolls through a stack of files and menus, and calls up security-cam video of the turbine.

He rewinds. He plays.

A grainy black-and-white video shows the monster turbine spinning freely.

Edison looks over Mr. Chimp's shoulder. "It's fine."

Mr. Chimp points to the time code in the upper left corner. One hour earlier.

Mr. Chimp fast-forwards.

The video image shows nothing but the turbine spinning.

"Fine, fine, fine," says Edison, suddenly more hopeful.

Then a shape, from the penstock feed, fills the right side of the screen.

Mr. Chimp punches PLAY.

"What?" says Edison.

A blurry figure, one blinking light on its head-shaped piece, hose arms snaking, legs kicking, dives headfirst into the turbine blades.

B I G R O B O T

"I know, I know," says Edison. "I can see as well as you."

Mr. Chimp shakes his head.

"But what is he doing? Robots shouldn't work under-water!"

On-screen, the grainy black-and-white Klank spreads his arms and legs and smashes the turbine as much as it smashes him. There is no sound, but the picture jumps with the force of metal on metal—pounding, bending, rip-ping, spinning, exploding into useless pieces.

Both turbine and robot fall to bits and wash out of the picture into the downstream outlet.

The turbine security-cam picture clears and shows—where there used to be a half-ton, steel-bladed turbine—nothing.

Edison stares at the empty screen.

"B-b-but what about my new lab? What about my money? What about my one and only power company? I mean, *our* company."

Mr. Chimp signs the obvious:

G     O     N     E

"OK, honey," Mrs. Edison calls from downstairs. "Dinner is ready. It's your favorite—fish!"

"Moooommmmm," whines Edison. "I hate fish."

"We don't say 'hate.' Now come down for dinner."

Mr. Chimp stands up. He looks back at the video screen. He shakes his head.

Mr. Chimp is sad that he will not get a new tire swing. Or his freedom.

But Mr. Chimp is a practical chimp. He has plenty more ideas.

"And, sweetie . . . ?"

"*What?*"

"Don't forget to scoop out the litter box."

Mr. Chimp rolls his eyes and hops up on the windowsill. He signs:

B  Y  E  –  B  Y  E

and jumps out the open window to the branch of the nearest tree.

FLOOOP, FLOOOP, FLOOOP.

**F**Grampa Al's windmill, beautifully reconstructed from a car's radiator fan, aluminum tent poles, a bicycle frame and chain, a rubber belt, pulleys, and plastic pipes, turns steadily in the brisk breeze on the roof of the old factory building.

"Smoother than a baby's butt," says Grampa Al.

Klink holds his windmill attachment up in the breeze and tops off his battery charge to full.

"Smoother than 'a flock of sheep that leisurely pass by one after one,'" says Klink.

Grampa Al stares, then laughs. "William Wordsworth? Did you just look that up?"

Klink nods his glass-domed head.

"You are turning into a real poet."

"And my feet show it!" says Klink. "They are Longfellows."

Grampa Al laughs even louder. "You have no idea why that's funny, do you?"

"Well," says Klink, "because long feet are . . . funny?"

"I didn't think so," says Grampa Al.

Watson loads a perfectly dimpled plastic pellet into his Perfect Peashooter. He takes aim at the empty soda can on the ledge. Puffs. Fires.

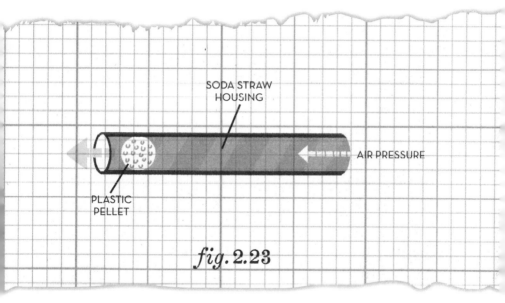

*fig.* **2.23**

*Plink!*

"Perfect," says Watson, without much enthusiasm.

Frank carefully places the Electro-Finger in its saxophone case.

Frank makes a last note in his Energy notebook and then closes it.

"Entry twenty-one," says Frank. "Tesla would have liked that. Seven times his favorite number, three."

Frank, Watson, and Grampa Al look out over the rooftops of downtown Midville. The sun sinks slowly below the western horizon. Streetlights and house lights wink on in the darkening dusk.

"I'm glad we could at least use the Electro-Finger to replace all the power generators Edison destroyed," says Frank.

"He would have controlled every bit of energy in Midville if it wasn't for Klank," says Watson. "I will remember Klank every time I see a light go on."

Klink, trying to think of something nice, and true, to say, is at least half successful. "I will remember Klank every time I think of electrons."

Frank shakes his head. "I thought I could put him back together. But there were just too many pieces. Too much was broken."

Frank flicks the trigger of the Electro-Finger back and forth.

*Flooop flooop flooop* goes Grampa Al's windmill, somehow sounding as sad as everyone feels.

*Flooop flooop flooop.* **Badang, badang, badang.**

The windmill sound turns into half Robot Boogie.

*Flooop* **badang** *flooop* **badang** *flooop* **badang badang badang.**

The guys turn away from the sunset to see what is going on with the windmill.

And there, shining in the last red rays of the setting sun, in all his repatched, reconstructed, crazy-new-added-parts, Robot Boogie–singing glory, is . . .

"Klank!" beeps truth-telling Klink.

"Klank?" says Watson.

"Klank . . . how?" asks Frank.

Grampa Al smiles. "I don't call this the Fix It! shop for nothing. Self-assembled . . . with a little Fix It! know-how."

Klank spreads his new arms. **"Hug!"**

Everyone piles into Klank for a scrum of human/robot hugs.

"Amazing," says Frank Einstein. "Klank is just like energy—he cannot be destroyed. Only changed to a different form!"

**"Badang badang badang. Badang a-lang a-ding dong. Boogie bing bong,"** electro-sound-wave–Robot-Boogies Klank.

Frank raises his Electro-Finger in the air and fires one beautiful, jagged, bright yellow bolt of pure electrical joy into the purpling clouds.

"We are happier than . . ."

"A pig in mud?" says Watson.

**"A chicken already across the road?"** adds Klank.

"Happier than a scientist, his best pal, his amazing grampa, and the two greatest robots ever," says Frank. "And we'll need all of us for our next challenge."

MATTER

ENERGY

HUMANS

Aristotle

Newton

$E = mc^2$

Tesla

Frank holds up a new notebook: HUMANS.

"The next category on our Wall of Science."

Watson nods. "Now, this should be more fun than—"

"—a cylinder-shaped wooden container with bulging sides full of small- to medium-sized primates that typically have tails and live in trees in tropical countries."

Everyone looks at Klink.

And laughs.

"Yes," says Frank Einstein. "Exactly."

# FRANK EINSTEIN'S ENERGY NOTES

**ENERGY**

Makes everything happen.

Without it, nothing can live or move.


**FORCES (USING ENERGY)**

Start things moving.

Change the way things move.

Stop things moving.

Hold everything together.

Break things apart.


**DIFFERENT KINDS OF ENERGY**

Light. Sound. Heat. Electric/magnetic. Mechanical.
Chemical. Nuclear.


**THE LAW OF ENERGY CONSERVATION**

Energy cannot be created or destroyed, only changed from
one form to another.

For example: sunlight –> grows tree –> burns wood –>
boils water –> steam turns turbine –> motion produces
electricity –> electricity heats coils –> coils toast bread –>
eaten toast gives muscles energy –> muscles move –>
movement makes action . . .

## HOW FORCES WORK

1. An object at rest will stay at rest (or straight line/constant speed) unless acted upon by an outside force.

2. The greater the force, the greater the change of motion of an object.

3. For every action, there is an equal and opposite reaction.

## FUNDAMENTAL FORCES

### GRAVITY

The force between bodies.

Makes objects fall, and holds planets in orbit.

### ELECTROMAGNETIC FORCE

Attracts negatively charged electrons to positively charged nucleus in the atom.

### STRONG NUCLEAR FORCE

Keeps protons and neutrons together in the atom's nucleus.

### WEAK NUCLEAR FORCE

Holds together bits that make up protons and neutrons.

## A WATSON FAVORITE INVENTION

People used to put sand and ash in cat litter boxes. Then one day in 1947, Ed Lowe's neighbor ran out of sand. Ed gave her clay because he knew clay would suck up more moisture and not be as messy as sand or ash.

The neighbor (and her cat) loved the clay.

So Ed filled bags with five pounds of clay to sell for sixty-five cents. And on the side of each bag, he wrote the name of his new invention: Kitty Litter.

## POEM IN POLICE CHIEF JACOBS'S POCKET

"POWER"
BY EMILY DICKINSON

You cannot put a fire out;
A thing that can ignite
Can go, itself, without a fan
Upon the slowest night.

You cannot fold a flood
And put it in a drawer, --
Because the winds would find it out,
And tell your cedar floor.

# KLINK AND KLANK MAKE PRESENT
## HOW TO MAKE YOUR OWN ELECTRO-FINGER

MATERIALS

Sheets of steel, aluminum, or any metal you can find

Copper wire

Buttons

Small LEDs

Switches

1 antenna

ASSEMBLY

Bend the metal into the shape of a glove.

Loop the wire into 357 perfect coils.

**"Why did it take the simple machine an hour to eat breakfast?"**

"Klank, we are explaining how to build an Electro-Finger. Do not interrupt."

Draw the magnetism of Earth inside the coils.

Move back and forth to gather electrons in—

**"It took a veeeeeeery long time."**

"What took a very long time?"

**"The simple machine's breakfast."**

"I told you I did not want to hear this."

**"OK. But . . . it is very funny."**

"No! Because we have only two pages to explain how to build an Electro-Finger, and if you insist on talking, we will not be able to fit all the instructions on these pages."

**"Because the orange-juice carton said concentrate!"**

"What?"

**"Ha-ha-ha!"**

"What?"

**"The orange-juice instructions said concentrate. Ha-ha-ha."**

"That is not funny."

**"So it took him a very long time to eat breakfast! Ha-ha-ha-ha-ha-ha-ha."**

"Noooooooooooooo bzzzzzzzz

zzzzzzzzzzzzzzzzzzzzzzzzz

zzzzzzzzzzzzzzzzzzzzzzzzz

zzzzzzzzzzzzzzzzzzzzzzzzz

zzzzzzzzzzzzzzzzzzzzzzzzzzz

zzzzzzzzzzzzzzzzzzzzzzzz

# A RECIPE FROM MR. CHIMP

**ANTS ON A LOG**

> 2 celery stalks, washed and trimmed
>
> 4 tablespoons peanut butter
>
> ½ cup ants (red or black)

> CUT the celery stalks in half.
>
> SPREAD peanut butter in each stalk.
>
> SPRINKLE the peanut butter with ants.

JON SCIESZKA has experimented with wireless electricity since birth, shocking the doctor who delivered him with a jolt of baby-JS static electricity. He is the author of *The True Story of the 3 Little Pigs!*, *The Stinky Cheese Man and Other Fairly Stupid Tales*, *Battle Bunny*, the Time Warp Trio series, and 4,832 other stories. He is the founder of Guys Read (a web-based literacy initiative for boys), and served as the first National Ambassador for Young People's Literature. He lives in Brooklyn, New York, and is still scientifically shocking.

BRIAN BIGGS has illustrated books by Garth Nix, Cynthia Rylant, and Katherine Applegate, and is the writer and illustrator of the Everything Goes series. He lives in Philadelphia.

PUBLISHER'S NOTE: THIS IS A WORK OF FICTION. NAMES, CHARACTERS, PLACES, AND INCI-
DENTS ARE EITHER THE PRODUCT OF THE AUTHOR'S IMAGINATION OR ARE USED FICTITIOUSLY,
AND ANY RESEMBLANCE TO ACTUAL PERSONS, LIVING OR DEAD, BUSINESS ESTABLISHMENTS,
EVENTS, OR LOCALES IS ENTIRELY COINCIDENTAL.

LIBRARY OF CONGRESS CATALOGING-IN-PUBLICATION DATA

SCIESZKA, JON.

FRANK EINSTEIN AND THE ELECTRO-FINGER / JON SCIESZKA ;

ILLUSTRATED BY BRIAN BIGGS.

PAGES CM. —— (FRANK EINSTEIN ; [2])

ISBN 978-1-4197-1483-2 (HARDCOVER) —— ISBN 978-1-61312-758-2 (EBOOK)

[1. ROBOTS——FICTION. 2. INVENTORS——FICTION. 3. POWER RESOURCES——FICTION. 4.
HUMOROUS STORIES. 5. SCIENCE FICTION.] I. BIGGS, BRIAN, ILLUSTRATOR. II. TITLE.

PZ7.S41267FS 2015

[FIC]——DC23

2014029591

ISBN FOR THIS EDITION: 978-1-4197-1666-9

TEXT COPYRIGHT © 2015 JON SCIESZKA

ILLUSTRATIONS COPYRIGHT © 2015 BRIAN BIGGS

BOOK DESIGN BY CHAD W. BECKERMAN

PRINTED AND BOUND IN U.S.A.

10 9 8 7 6 5 4 3 2 1

AMULET BOOKS ARE AVAILABLE AT SPECIAL DISCOUNTS WHEN PURCHASED IN QUANTITY FOR
PREMIUMS AND PROMOTIONS AS WELL AS FUNDRAISING OR EDUCATIONAL USE. SPECIAL
EDITIONS CAN ALSO BE CREATED TO SPECIFICATION. FOR DETAILS, CONTACT SPECIALSALES@
ABRAMSBOOKS.COM OR THE ADDRESS BELOW.

ABRAMS

161-165 FARRINGDON ROAD
LONDON, UK ECIR 3AL
WWW.ABRAMSANDCHRONICLE.CO.UK

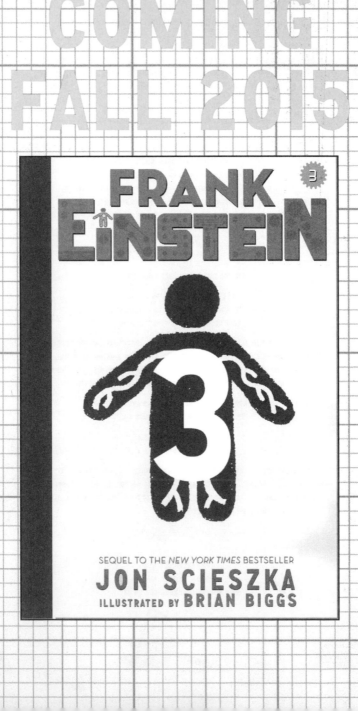

COMING
FALL 2015

FRANK EINSTEIN

3

3

SEQUEL TO THE *NEW YORK TIMES* BESTSELLER
JON SCIESZKA
ILLUSTRATED BY BRIAN BIGGS